THE AUTHOR

A FAIRY TALE
BASED ON A TRUE STORY

By Evelyne Day Rush

 FriesenPress

Suite 300 - 990 Fort St
Victoria, BC, V8V 3K2
Canada

www.friesenpress.com

Copyright © 2019 by Evelyne Day Rush
First Edition — 2019

Attention: quantity discounts are available to your company, educational institution or writing organisation for reselling, educational purposes, subscription incentives, gifts or fundraiser campaigns.
For further information please contact the Author directly:
evelynedayrush@gmail.com

ISBN
978-1-5255-4697-6 (Hardcover)
978-1-5255-4698-3 (Paperback)
978-1-5255-4699-0 (eBook)

1. Fiction, Coming Of Age

Distributed to the trade by The Ingram Book Company

DEDICATION

I would like to thank my mother, who has always been there for me. Mom, you have always listened and refrained from judgement even when I was at my worst. You are the best mom in the whole world. I love you deeply.

I would also like to thank my husband. Honey, you truly are the perfect husband for me. You are my knight in shining armour, my very own musketeer, and my Prince Charming. You always make me feel like a princess. You are pleasant to be with. You are an extraordinary father to our children and you are my love eternally. I love you, darling.

ACKNOWLEDGEMENTS

I would like to thank my friend Francine Girard, designer and owner of Vestita.ca, for the red top.

I would also like to thank my friend and photographer Andrea Johnstone for taking my picture.

You two made me look like a million bucks!
Thank you!

CHILDHOOD IN THE COUNTRY

Her eyelids were heavy. Trying to open them was difficult, as if each one weighed 200 pounds. Her first attempt failed halfway. A second try gained a glance at part of the white, empty wall in front of her—then darkness again.

Her entire body was paralyzed; moving required too much effort. She had no strength left in her. She felt her heart thumping like a bass drum on her bed. It was a fast, rhythmic sound. Where was she? The previous night was a blur.

A familiar sound helped jog her memory: the ringing of her apartment door buzzer. Her third attempt to open her eyes ended in another failure. The buzzer rang again, but this time as a long, continuous sound that reminded her of the elementary school recess bell. She passed out while an echo of the bell mixed with children talking over each other filled her head.

"Quiet, children. Recess is over; I need to talk to you all," Eva's teacher said with an annoyed tone. It was clear that Mrs. Potts did not want to have this talk with her pupils. However, after a conversation with one of the parents the evening before, she could no longer keep quiet about the activities she had witnessed more than once in the schoolyard. She had clearly misinterpreted what she first perceived as innocent children's games. Some of her grade four students were behaving inappropriately.

The night before, a boy had come home with a bleeding lip, and his parent had informed Mrs. Potts that a girl was the culprit. Apparently, she had bitten him on the lips while trying to kiss him. Mrs. Potts was determined to stop this by talking to her young students.

She stood tall beside her chair, her yellow hair up in a bun. Her black reading glasses hung from the tip of her nose, accentuating the seriousness of her face, which, along with her solemn tone, contrasted with her colourful clothes. She would have been less impressive if she had not worn the big platform shoes, which matched her rust-coloured jeans and orange shirt with white polka dots and was half hidden by her hand-knitted beige vest. Mrs. Potts was trying hard to be in fashion; however, her 1970s elephant pants did not suit her 1950s hairstyle, and her countenance contradicted her efforts.

Forced to listen, Eva squirmed in her seat and chuckled with discomfort. She longed for her teacher to end the talk and move on to another subject. Any subject sounded better than this. Even the dreaded topic of mathematics would have been less painful. The more Mrs. Potts talked about how the kissing and hugging in the corner of the schoolyard was inappropriate and should be stopped and that punishment for such behaviour was guaranteed if caught, the more Eva squirmed and chuckled uneasily.

Having failed to muffle another chuckle while thinking about raising her hand to ask permission to go to the bathroom in an effort to escape what felt like torture, Mrs. Potts looked directly at her. "Stop laughing, Eva Day Rush. I'm talking about you!"

All the other children laughed mockingly. Mrs. Potts quieted the class and then moved on to the blessed subject of mathematics.

For Eva, subtractions became a noise in the background. Now everyone knew she had kissed a boy. Worst of all, they knew she had bitten him in the process. She felt shame and guilt. What would her friends say? What would the other boys think of her? Had they not just laughed at her? If what she thought was hidden was now revealed, would they find out her other secret, the one secret no one knew about?

Somehow, the weeks that followed did not turn out the way she thought. She dreaded the mockery or, worse, the shunning. However, some girls started to ask her questions about how it felt to kiss a boy. Their timidity prevented them from daring to ask for a kiss. They were also too shy to allow a boy to kiss them. Some other girls kept their distance, but Eva didn't care about them. She was enjoying her newfound popularity too much, including the growing crowd around her. She did not attend to those who shrank away.

Girls were not the only ones fattening the flock; some boys were also lured in. Most boys Eva's age couldn't care less about girls. Playing hockey or kicking a soccer ball was much more interesting than wasting time kissing girls. But for the few boys who were part of her inner circle, Eva was captivating and attractive. They stuck to her like metal to a magnet. Kisses on the cheek and occasional pecks on the mouth were exchanged, along with bracelets, necklaces, and even little rings. She loved the attention, and the gifts were a perk. Being popular was addictive.

By the beginning of grade six, she felt grown up. Being part of the oldest group in the school helped. She relished the role as eldest and enjoyed having been the most popular girl at North Side Elementary (NSE) School for two years in a row. For her last year, she planned to maintain her popularity status at all costs.

North Side Elementary was a small building with only two floors. Its large asphalt front yard compensated for its size. Cornfields pressed in on the other three sides. The school looked like a two-storey boat in the middle of a sea of corn. The main entrance was perfectly symmetrical in front of the yard. The gym was central to the school. Lockers furnished three walls, and the fourth side held a small but practical stage. Lunch tables were folded and stacked, one next to the other, waiting to be unfolded each noonday, transforming the gym into a cafeteria. Teachers' and staff offices were adjacent to the gym. Classes were on the second floor. All students resided on either the north or south side of Myerbell, as Myerbell County was divided in two. However, all children from the north side only attended NSE.

The north side was filled with wooded land and corn or wheat fields. Its population consisted mainly of farmers. The town was located on the south side. It was large enough to have three elementary schools and one large high school: Myerbell High. Only thirty minutes from the metropolis of Real Mountain, Myerbell was a proud town.

Eva lived on a hobby farm on the north side of town. Her parents owned a few cows, some rabbits, and several chickens—not to mention several cats, a dog, and a hamster. Eva enjoyed the animals. She would run in the cornfields with her little white dog, Peanut, at her side and climb trees. She did not like weeding the garden, but it was a small price to pay to get to swim for hours in their swimming pool and ride her bicycle on the long, empty, quiet country road. Country life had its advantages.

Her parents were devoutly religious, and Sundays revolved around church attendance. Eva loved the smell of incense and regularly served the priest at the altar during mass. On a few occasions, her mom brought her to the nuns' convent for special mass. Eva loved the peace that filled the convent and was inspired by the beautiful crystalline voices of the nuns' choir.

Eva would often pray to for her "secret" to go away. But every morning, she would awake to the sad reality that her prayers had gone unanswered. The urine smell and the discomfort of the wet bedsheets brought her shame and embarrassment. Even though she was way too old for this, she woke up every morning as if she had slept in a bog.

There were few houses around where Eva lived—only four little girls she might play with lived within walking distance. For Eva, girls held no mystery. She had played show-and-tell in the past. However, it had been more like show-and-touch. They would do a countdown, at the end of which they would quickly lift their shirt to flash their naked chests. That was one game. The other was to touch (and sometimes more than the top part) the other girls body. After a couple of summer afternoons playing these games, Eva realized that all girls were built pretty much the same way—what she saw in the mirror every day was what all the other girls saw. There was no more thrill of the unknown. Eva had also seen her mother naked a few times. Having always been honest with Eva, her mother had not shied away from informing Eva of the transformation her body would soon experience.

Eva's father, on the other hand, was a reserved man. He worked in town during the day and farmed in the evening, and was seldom in the house. When he was, he kept to himself, sitting in front of the television. The least dressed Eva ever saw him was when he wore his green-and-blue-striped cotton housecoat, which fully covered him. Even when swimming in their pool, he wore orange shorts with a matching button-up shirt that covered him from neck to knees. Eva loved her parents and felt their love in return, but her curiosity for everything that life could bring was overbearing.

Her parents did not do much besides work and take care of her, and Eva did not want that for herself. She had a deep desire for adventure, fun, and excitement. The calm of the country was often mixed with boredom. Her popularity with boys at NSE and her numerous girlfriends did not change her mindset. Her opinion of herself was clear: she considered herself boring and unattractive, because anything or anyone coming from the north was unappealing. The shame of her secret enhanced her negative self-image.

Her fascination with the town was like a spell. That's why she preferred to hang around the south-side kids. She considered her town friends richly advantaged and wanted a part of what they had to offer. It was as if her friends had something that she did not, a power Eva desired. She considered them cool and wanted to be like them. She wanted to hang around them, so she could feel cool too. Cool meant attractive, popular, and important.

On a normal Thursday, while everyone was in their classroom learning all kinds of interesting new things, Eva requested a bathroom break, to which her teacher agreed. As she turned the corner of the last set of stairs, she saw Mr. Bieler, the gym teacher, exiting the girls' bathroom, evidently heading toward the principal's office.

Puzzled, Eva walked toward the girls' bathroom. As she was about to open the door, it opened from the inside, almost hitting her in the forehead. With a whirl of fury, Edith, a south-side girl, burst out and ran back to class, murmuring unrepeatable words without even acknowledging Eva. Mr. Bieler had caught her smoking a cigarette while sitting on the toilet. Her shame and embarrassment were noticeable in her red cheeks, which contrasted with her pale face. Edith was a sickly looking girl with skin so white she looked like a ghost. Her stride, however, was anything but weak.

That evening, Eva was on the phone listening to Edith's side of the story. She said Mr. Bieler had peeked in the girls' bathroom to look at her peeing. "That guy is a pervert," she said, outraged. That night, the telephone game did its magic. Edith told a friend, who told a friend, who told a friend. By the next morning, most grade six students had been part of the telephone tag and had heard that Mr. Bieler was a peeping Tom. However, strangely enough, Edith was absent.

During lunch, the principal walked onto the stage of the converted gymnasium. He looked at the students without a word, expecting his presence on the platform would be enough for all to stop talking. His hair was parted on one side, the longest hair trying to reach the other side of his head in a failed attempt to hide his baldness. His brown suit was tight at the hips, choking his groin like a corset, and his bell-bottom pants hid his platform shoes. His open suit coat revealed his overgrown potbelly.

"Ahem!" he began. "We would like to reiterate, particularly to the grade six students, that smoking in the bathrooms, or anywhere in the school or on the school grounds, is strictly prohibited."

Everyone listened in deafening silence.

"Anyone caught smoking will face a one-day suspension. Mr. Bieler caught someone yesterday, and we want to inform you that she is currently serving her punishment. Thank you for your attention."

As the principal exited the stage by the side stairs, chewing noises, forks clacking against plates, and student voices reached a crescendo. Everyone had an opinion on the subject, each expressing it on the sly. No one dared to defy authority for fear of reprimand.

The afternoon seemed endless. Eva would have to wait until evening for her next phone conversation with Edith, because waiting for Monday morning to speak to her in person would be intolerable.

That night, Eva consoled Edith, and the girls agreed that teachers, principals, and parents were so old fashioned. "They understand nothing. It was just a stupid little cigarette," Edith said.

That weekend, Eva experienced like never before the feeling of isolation from living in the country. She was awakened to a new way of viewing her home. The dichotomy was clear. She liked the animals and the surrounding nature, but because she could only see her south-side friends at school, she felt imprisoned. There was no public bus service for residents of the north. The buses only ran in town, which meant Eva was dependant on her mother or father to go anywhere. And they thought Eva was too young to be left alone at a stranger's place or to get rides from people they did not know. Eva felt stuck. Never had the country felt so imprisoning.

Now that she was entering her teen years as well as her graduating year, she considered ways to escape through extra-curricular activities. She wanted to join the girls' hockey team, but her dad said hockey was too dangerous for his little girl, and forbade her to play.

Then there was the downhill ski club. Eva thought her parents would be thrilled to enrol her since one of her neighbour friends was entering the club, and her friend's parents offered to drive Eva with them, which meant no carpooling for her parents. "No! It's too dangerous to ski downhill, my darling," her father had replied. Eva had turned on her heel and headed to her bedroom, huffing and puffing with anger.

It seemed like her father found everything dangerous. She hated it. Her bedroom felt like it was closing in on her. She was suffocating. Eva's escape of choice was writing in her diary. She wrote what she would have liked to tell her father but could not. Making sure she locked the book with a key, she kept it safe between clothes in one of her wardrobe drawers.

What was acceptable for the Day Rush household was singing in the choir, playing the piano or guitar, or engaging in the school debate club. Those were all "safe" activities. Eva learned the piano for eighteen months and then became bored with practicing. Playing on the upright antique piano was fun as long as it was only for a few minutes at a time. Her teacher told her mother that there was no point pursuing classes if Eva did not practice at home.

Declaring piano was the problem, Eva pleaded to learn the guitar. But after six months, that no longer held any interest for her either. She claimed the strings hurt too much and so was released from further classes.

Eva had maintained her interest in oral debate for a few years; however, the club was exclusively for elementary students, and she would have needed to move to Real Mountain to pursue that field. Although the thought of living in the city thrilled her, Eva did not insist, since she did not have any power over a move of such magnitude. Deep down she did not have a real passion for it anyway. It seemed like anything she was allowed to do did not interest her. The pull to get involved in forbidden activities became stronger every day, and her father unwittingly contributed to it.

One school night when she should have been in bed, Eva was talking on the phone with her best friend.

Natasha was a short, plump redhead who attended drama class after school at a private studio. She was a joyful, levelheaded girl, and the buddies were frank with each other, able to be themselves. Their telephone conversations were always a welcome diversion for Eva, and that night was no exception.

Sitting in her parents' bedroom where the telephone was located, Eva had been talking for over an hour when her father complained that she needed to hang up to free up the line. Eva ignored him and continued her conversation. After a second warning from her father, who stood on the other side of the door threatening to hang up himself if she did not obey right away, Eva persisted in her small talk.

Then it happened. In a fit of rage, Eva's father broke down the door with his shoulder. Eva had never seen him so angry. As she saw the doorframe broken in pieces, she feared him for the first time.

She ended her conversation abruptly, hung up, and ran to her bedroom, slamming the door behind her. With her body shaking like a leaf in the wind, she pushed her bed against her door in an effort to prevent her father from being able to open it. What she wrote in her diary that night did not reflect the childhood values she had learned at home or in church.

Eva longed for the day when she would be free to be alone with her friends. Little did she realize her situation was about to change during the summer following her grade six graduation.

2

MYERBELL HIGH AND MIGHTY

Eva would be thirteen that summer, and her parents considered her old enough to spend some time alone in town. Finally, Eva could hang around town without her parents.

One day, her mom agreed to drop her at the park for a few hours while she ran errands. Eva secretly joined Edith and Natasha. Edith was the instigator, who plotted with the other two girls for a clandestine gathering with three boys. *Three couples would be quite fun*, Eva thought. At the count of three, they would all kiss their mate, and it would not be a peck on the cheek. For the first time, Eva was going to give a real French kiss.

Eva was matched with Henrick, as Edith had already decided who was going to kiss whom. Henrick was a short, dark-haired boy who was in serious need of orthodontics—his buckteeth were quite impressive. But Eva didn't mind. She had someone from the south side who liked her enough to give her a real French kiss, and that was all that mattered. Rolling their tongues together made her feel mature and grown up, like a woman. The fact that their teeth banged together and that a little drool leaked out of his mouth was not important. She had French-kissed a boy; therefore, she was ready to enter junior high.

That summer, something else happened, something that enabled the leap from childhood to womanhood.

On a hot summer afternoon, Eva was reading comic books outside on the hammock. The warm wind was gently blowing on the tree leaves, and the rocking of her hammock was relaxing. In that beautiful setting, Eva experienced the beginning of her physical transformation from child to adult. She felt something leaking gently from her. She went to the bathroom, only to find her panties were stained with something reddish and brown. She was not surprised; she knew what it was. Her mom had told her all about womanhood, periods, and how babies were made. She was well prepared. She simply took a sanitary napkin from the cupboard, placed it where it belonged, and that was the end of it.

Eva appeared to be calm, mature, and poised that evening at the dinner table. However, inside, she was ecstatic. She considered herself to be truly a woman now that her own body was testifying to her exit from childhood.

Back at her apartment, all the beautiful country faded from her mind as Eva slowly woke up. The birds singing and the gentle sound of the wind blowing in the leaves vanished like a vapour as the city noises forced her out of her slumber.

Eva opened her eyes again to the same white, empty wall. This time they opened fully. She recognized her bedroom: undecorated, absent of pictures, and poorly furnished. The canvas blind, which was too short for the window, partially hid the bright sun. Its rays infiltrated the bottom of the window. Eva grunted and rolled over onto her other side. Even though the door buzzer stopped, she could still hear someone outside. She heard a thump and the shuffling of plastic and then heavy footsteps leaving. *Good riddance,* she thought. Getting up was not part of her plan, and she allowed herself to drift back to sleep.

High school was exhilarating. All the children from the three elementary schools were gathered in one huge place. Since NSE was the smallest of the three, the number of students at Myerbell High was close to 2,000.

Myerbell High was vibrant in activities, each more inviting than the last. To have teachers who did not know her would allow for a clean slate. Mrs. Potts's grade four ordeal had created a reputation for her amongst the other teachers, and it had followed her through grades five and six.

Long gone were the days when she stood in a line to enter or exit the classroom. She had been the tallest in her class during her elementary years, and she welcomed the freedom to walk where she wanted without having to wait for everyone else to get in front of her. She had the responsibility to get to her designated class on time or else face the consequences.

The best part of Myerbell High was the boys. It was obvious that most of them had also undergone changes during the summer. For some, their voices were different. Others had what looked like the beginning of beards or moustaches growing on their face.

Watching the change in the boys' physical appearance over the last three months had been exciting. Henrick and his buckteeth no longer interested her as she noticed other boys who were better looking.

The first one who melted Eva's heart was Nolan. He was tall and his newly grown sparse moustache made him look older than he was. Being a sociable person, he engaged in a conversation with her on the first day of school. He liked to dance and offered to show her some moves. She joyfully agreed.

Then there was Mark. He made Eva laugh. He often had funny jokes and usually came to school with his skateboard. He displayed infinite patience while showing Eva how to use it. Mark was dark haired as well, and his physique displayed newly formed muscles that were pleasing to the eye. His voice had deepened dramatically over the summer, and listening to him gave her a thrill. Mark's best friend was Lewis.

He walked as if he owned the world. He looked like he was so sure of himself. That assurance was magnetic for Eva. She found Lewis mysterious and intriguing. He was also buff and athletic. His light-brown, shoulder-length hair and blue eyes got the attention of all the girls. He knew it, and he liked it. Winning some trophies and medals for participating in various sporting events made him popular with the boys too. Having Lewis in the team almost guaranteed a win. Plus, hanging out with him gained the girls' attention.

On the first day of school, Natasha met Eva at the main gates. The girls had kept in touch throughout the summer and were as close as friends could be. Exploring the huge complex caused several "ohhhs" and "awwws!" The psychedelic art decorating the walls fit right in with the early days of the '80s. Disco music coming from boom boxes resounded through the seemingly endless halls, which went from one complex to another. The few students who owned them stood out, attracting small crowds of curious spectators.

There was a gym complex with an indoor pool—half the size of an Olympic pool—and a huge gymnasium that was spacious enough to play hockey or football with ease. The gym could also be separated into three smaller spaces by metal shutters, each one big enough for a tennis court. The school also had a mechanics complex, where all the special education students attended. Natasha and Eva agreed they would never cross the threshold of that complex for fear of being perceived as special education students themselves. That would have been an instant coolness killer.

The huge cafeteria was used exclusively for eating. The atrium attracted different gangs as a hangout place. The ceiling of the cafeteria and atrium was impressively high, the equivalent of two storeys. The school also had two biology labs, a photo lab, a literature and languages wing, and a library.

Since there was no library at NSE, discovering such a wonderfully filled library at Myerbell High School made the girls all bubbly and giggly. The smell of the new books was intoxicating. The new carpet with its matching furniture reflected the latest fashions of the new era and created an ambiance that both girls enjoyed. The chairs were comfortable. The television screens for viewing VHS or Beta movies and the selection of films and documentaries would have made anyone drool with envy. The library also had music on cassette tapes and albums. Using a headset, students could listen as long as they wished—during recess, of course.

A scrawny redheaded boy with freckles on his cheeks was sitting alone. His big beige plastic-framed glasses magnified his eyes to gargantuan proportion. Jimmy was reading a science book, surrounded by piles of other books, each thicker than the last. Edith was in a far corner, making eyes at Lewis, who pretended not to notice. Sitting next to him was Mark, who was whispering in Lewis's ear. Failing to squelch their laughter, they received a disapproving look from the librarian.

Mrs. Greenick was clear when it came to library rules and regulations: no noise was tolerated whatsoever. Anyone caught breaking the rules was presented the door without warning. In her opinion, the signs posted throughout the library and on the door were warning enough. Mrs. Greenick reminded Eva of Mrs. Potts. She also looked like she came straight from a 1950s magazine. However, Mrs. Greenick did not try to be in fashion; she just wore 1950s clothes. Her grey hair was tucked into a bun, and she wore her pointed glasses at all times. They made her look severe and inflexible. Eva and Natasha learned soon enough that she not only looked severe and inflexible, she was.

For the first few weeks, Eva felt safe in the ocean of people. The anonymity it brought reassured her that the mistakes and childish foolishness of her elementary years were gone for good.

Although all the familiar faces from her elementary years were present, there were so many new faces that, at first, she clung to Natasha like a leech. However, they did not have all their classes together, which forced Eva to make new friends.

Eva had a one-track mind: fitting in. More than that, she wanted to fit in with the "in" crowd. She wanted to be cool and popular. More than anything, she wanted a boyfriend. Therefore, sticking around old NSE friends was not the solution. Except for Natasha and Edith, Eva was determined to change friends and be part of the popular group. But her secret was holding her back. She was afraid it would be revealed, and the humiliation would kill her.

Ever since her lip-biting event in grade four, Eva had begun to think differently. Her perception of who she was and where she lived changed. She began to think that town folks were cool and country folks were not and that her secret made her different in a bad way, and that she would never fit in because of it. Even though she had many friends, and boys liked her, she perceived herself as not cool enough for a south-side boy to make her his girlfriend. Her perception increased throughout the years, to the point of believing she was nothing without a boyfriend. No boyfriend meant she was ugly, unlovable, and unworthy. Eva vowed to get a boyfriend to prove to everyone—most importantly herself—that she was beautiful, attractive, and worthy. She was not sure where she heard all that or who had said it, but she did not bother to challenge the thoughts, convinced they were true.

One Monday morning, like everybody else around her, Eva was walking frantically up the stairs to her first class of the day. Her teachers did not tolerate lateness. As Eva reached the last step, she felt something brush against her bum. She turned around to see Lewis and Mark three stairs below, their heads bent toward her bum as they smelled it. When they realized they had been caught, they straightened up and walked past her as if nothing had happened. Driven by their newly discovered testosterone, they were checking to see who was a woman and who was not, who had experienced Eva's transformation and who had not, as if her newly formed breasts were not proof enough. Eva did not know what to think. Part of her was proud that she was one of those who had transitioned from childhood to womanhood, but part of her felt uncomfortable to have been sniffed like a dog.

Fall turned into winter, and biology class became increasingly interesting. In one class, they dissected giant grasshoppers from Africa. The smell of formalin overpowered the room, and the sight of grasshopper cadavers was nauseating.

"What's that smell?" Lewis asked in an attempt to get some attention.

"I feel sick to my stomach, Mrs. Applebee. Can I go to the bathroom?" Edith added loudly in the hopes of being noticed by Lewis.

Mrs. Applebee, a short lady with short black hair who always wore a long white lab coat, replied with a sigh that it was OK for anyone who did not want to dissect a grasshopper to skip class. Half the room emptied within minutes, boys and girls leaving in disgust.

As if Mrs. Applebee had not learned her lesson, she led another class on dissection a few weeks later, this time with mice. In Eva's mind, dissecting an insect was fine. She had joined the half who stayed behind and went ahead with analyzing the grasshopper's body parts. However, she refused to be part of it this time. It was one thing to dissect a grasshopper, but it was another to dissect a cute little furry friend. The mice reminded her of her beige hamster at home. She did not want to see the blood and guts.

Shortly after Christmas holidays, it seemed as if there was some sort of stratagem against the biology students between Mrs. Applebee and Mr. Coltman, the junior high gym teacher. The two accomplices declared the boys would head to the gym with Mr. Coltman for a talk, and the girls would stay in class with Mrs. Applebee. The scheme was on the topic of the birds and the bees, and neither teacher wanted to embarrass their students with facts concerning the other gender. In fact, students wanted to know all about the other gender and secretly wished to be in the other classroom.

The girls got a pink book on ovulation and pregnancy in layperson's terms, and the boys got some books on mechanics and cars. At least that's what the cover of the booklet looked like from Eva's seat across from Mark in the cafeteria.

Eva was curious to know what the boys were told, and the booklet looked interesting, but she was too shy to ask for a copy. She was not even sure if the teacher would have given her one.

When Lewis laughed at Mark for having a copy in his hand, saying it was stupid to read such a boring booklet, it stopped Eva in her tracks. She brushed off the desire and prevented herself from entertaining the thought of getting one. Lewis was cool and macho. He knew about things and talked about them openly. While the other guys and girls listened, their naiveté and ignorance were exposed. Lewis narrated things in a vulgar, offensive way. He knew how to captivate his audience. His way of telling about the birds and the bees was certainly different from the teachers, and for inquisitive thirteen-year-olds, Lewis was much more interesting than the official biology class version they had just heard.

Winter was long and cold, and Valentine's Day was approaching fast. To counter the winter blues, Mr. Coltman took it upon himself to teach karate. Eva was a fast learner, and she enjoyed the sense of strength that learning self-defence brought.

To get graded, Mr. Coltman informed his students that they would be paired up in teams of two to demonstrate the various moves they learned in class. Eva was matched with Jimmy. Jimmy was smart. He was at the top of his class in every subject except gym. His voice had not changed during the summer or the fall, and there were definitely no signs of moustache growth anytime soon.

Eva stood on one corner of the carpet and Jimmy on the opposite side. They looked at each other and then took a few steps forward. The rest of the class sat around the four corners of the thick blue carpet, which was the size of a boxing ring. As the other students watched, the boys encouraged Jimmy, and the girls cheered on Eva.

The opponents locked arms, each grabbing the other's sleeves. Jimmy tried to make Eva fall by doing a foot manoeuvre, but Eva swung him to the floor within seconds. All the students laughed at Jimmy for his quick demise and for the fact that his conqueror was a girl.

Mr. Coltman intervened and ended the commotion to Eva's disappointment. She was proud of her accomplishment, almost surprised at herself. However, she soon realized that the boys were not impressed with her prowess.

Valentine's Day came without a valentine for Eva. She thought it was because she had beaten Jimmy, and that scared away the boys. She figured the boys thought she wasn't pretty or sexy enough, that she was not worth being a Valentine to anyone, that she was just some country girl, uncool and therefore unattractive. Eva felt emptiness inside. Her way of thinking was reinforced by her conclusion that beating boys at karate was certainly not a way to get a boyfriend.

Winter gave way to spring, and Eva's struggles to fit in grew. Nolan was helping and made her feel special, but Eva was no longer interested in him.

Nolan had seemed like a nice guy at the beginning of the year, but as the months went by, she'd realized the other boys didn't hold Nolan in high regard. They mocked his dancing skills, and hanging around him felt like social suicide to Eva. Part of her liked Nolan, but her desire to be popular was so overpowering that she preferred not to be around him too often.

A battle was raging inside. While she recognized that Nolan had only been kind and respectful toward her, she was reluctant to hang out with him because Nolan was not cool, according to the popular kids at school. She despised herself. She hated something inside her that she could not even define. She felt condemned by herself. The hatred came from how she was thinking. She hated herself to the point of hating life altogether.

Thinking there was no other way out, she concocted a plan that would crush the inner battle. Almost immediately, she felt the equivalent of an internal ceasefire.

3

GRADE EIGHT FATALITIES

On a Friday afternoon toward the end of May, the first signs of summer appeared. A warm wind blew gently on Eva's long black hair, reaching her thin, narrow hips. At the ring of the bell, indicating the end of the last recess, instead of returning to class, Eva took a knife and stayed outside. Alone in the deserted schoolyard, sitting on the ground in a secluded area, she started to cut her skinny wrist. She wanted to stop the pain, to end the battle in her mind. Part of her wanted to be friends with Nolan. She knew him to be a good person. But she kept thinking about how uncool Nolan was and how hanging around him would make her look bad. The internal battle raged furiously in her head and heart. Eva just wanted it to stop.

But her thought process kept on. *Either way, you'll never be cool enough to be attractive to anyone,* her mind said. *Think about your secret. You're too skinny, and your breasts aren't big enough. You look like a two-by-four.*

As tiny drops of blood started to dribble to the ground, she felt nauseous and tried to stop the bleeding with her gym shirt, which she pulled out of her backpack. Because the cuts were superficial, they went unnoticed. Unable to go through with her suicide attempt, she spent the end of the school year uneventfully. However, life at home became intolerable for Eva that summer.

Eva's father grew increasingly distant. She understood him less and less, and her desire to please him was fading. He would sit in front of the TV and watch his shows every night of the week. As a child, Eva had loved to sit with her father and watch hockey games until bedtime. However, hockey season was over, and sitcoms replaced any family communication. No one would dare interrupt him while he was watching. If anyone—Eva or her mother—made noise while the TV was on, he would tell the disruptive culprit to keep quiet. No subject matter was more important than his TV shows, and anything could wait for the commercials. However, commercials were for bathroom breaks or fetching a snack.

During weekends, he would alternate between spending an hour cutting grass and another hour drinking beer. Whether it was feeding the cows, cleaning the chicken pen, or performing pool maintenance, he alternated between the activity and drinking. Eva would have loved to help him with those chores, but whenever she offered, he would remind her that such activities were too difficult for her, that she could get hurt doing them, and that it was his role as her father to do them.

Eva had never seen her father get drunk to the point of behaving inappropriately. He would go to bed as soon as he had a little too much. However, she had heard him say hurtful words while sober. Giving him a gift was a toilsome task and often ended up with a criticism as a thank you.

His favourite meal was French baguettes with European cheese and foie gras, which were always accompanied with many bottles of wine. Eva's mom had introduced him to it when they were newlyweds, and he loved it so much that it increasingly became part of the menu, particularly on Saturday nights. Eva's parents said she was too young to drink alcohol. So, she partook in the meal while watching her parents drink.

It was during one of those favourite meals that summer that Eva dared to ask her parents if she could have a glass of wine. In a heartbeat, her father responded that she was too young to drink and that he would determine when she could have her first glass. Eva swallowed her anger, took a piece of bread, and ate it while having an argument with him in her mind, thinking of everything she wished she had the courage to tell him.

"He can't see that I've grown and matured, and he's still treating me like a child. I'm not a baby anymore. Doesn't he get it? Is he blind or something?" Eva signed the last line of her journal page with "The Black Sheep." She felt like a black sheep. She was the cause of frequent arguments between her mother and father, and that made her feel worse.

Her return to school in the fall was both welcomed and dreaded. Welcomed because it would separate her from her parents for most of the day, dreaded because of the hole inside her. Her longing to be loved and accepted was growing at an uncontrollable rate. It was stinging, irritating, and nauseating all at once. As much as Eva's desire to fit in swelled like a cancerous tumour, she found solace in her flourishing friendship with Natasha. They hung out together on a regular basis.

Besides journaling, Eva escaped with music. She loved music class at school. The fact that she had learned the piano and guitar in elementary school made her stand out from the rest of the class. Her music teacher was a gentleman in his late seventies, and she loved him dearly. He was gentle, kind, and respectful. He had been in a concentration camp during the war and had used music to survive. His full head of white hair and clear blue eyes revealed that he must have been handsome as a young man. Eva loved to listen to him tell stories of past times.

One time he expressed his disappointment over the students' test results. He stated with a tone that betrayed his sadness that the entire class had failed, except for Eva, who had achieved a mark of 85%. He added that Eva would receive an award for her accomplishment. Eva could sense how disappointed he was at the other students and how proud he was of her. She did not know how to feel. Part of her felt honoured and joyful for her mark but another part felt ashamed because she was standing out. She was not fitting in! Surely, the others would be jealous of her. She could almost hear them in her head: *Teacher's pet, teacher's pet, teacher's pet.*

Her next class was literature, and Eva was annoyed at having to wait. Her teacher had not arrived yet, and she was bored. As she daydreamed, gazing at the empty wall to her left, her head leaning on her right arm, she caught herself sucking the upper part, creating a red mark.

"*Look!*" she said to Edith, who was sitting in front of her. "*I made a red mark.*"

Edith had changed dramatically from the two summers before. She no longer looked sickly. Although her skin was still pale, her hair was longer and blonder than ever. Coupled with the growth of an impressive chest, she was attracting boys like bees to honey.

"Look, everyone," Edith replied mockingly, loud enough for everyone to hear. "Eva gave herself a hickey!"

Everyone laughed. Eva learned a painful lesson that day about what a love bite was. *You're an imbecile,* she told herself, hating her naiveté. She had done it again: stood out because of her stupidity. She hated herself more and more. She was not fitting in.

Eva was bored again during recess. To get rid of her boredom and accompanying loneliness, she sat down in the cafeteria at a table of newly acquainted friends. The conversation turned to balloons and parties. Some were saying how they loved red balloons and others blue ones. They also mentioned clown and horse-shaped balloons of all sizes.

"I once saw a clear balloon in the shape of a banana," Eva announced. Everyone exploded in laughter. Not understanding what was so funny, Eva just sat there looking puzzled.

"She doesn't even know what a condom is!" a girl sitting nearby said, which only caused everyone to laugh even louder.

You're beyond stupid, she told herself as she sat there pretending it was funny while her insides swirled with pain.

The next day, Eva sat at another table, as far as possible from her new acquaintances, hoping they would forget her. As she lifted her bland, pink food tray to ensure the seat was clean, a boy passed by and grabbed her change, which was beside her plate on her tray.

"Hey, that's mine!" she protested.

The boy merely smirked at her. "Prove it."

As he left, proclaiming for everyone to hear that he had not taken her money, Eva stood there, powerless. There was nothing she could do. That was the last time she would leave money in plain sight.

You idiot! she thought. *Not only do you look like a fool, you are one.* She sat alone, eating her meal while suppressing her tears.

During archery class, Eva was bored yet again. Waiting for her turn to use the equipment seemed like an eternity. As she sat on the narrow wooden bench along the wall, she eavesdropped on a conversation between two classmates who were also waiting their turn. One girl was pondering what it would feel like to be at the receiving end of a bow and arrow.

When it was Eva's turn to practice her archery skills, she took the bow and arrow and, without drawing the string, pointed it at the girl. "Now you know," she said.

The girl screamed, as did their gym teacher. "Eva, get out of the class! You're suspended for dangerous behaviour. I don't want to see you again until next week."

Eva did not even have time to reassure the girl or the teacher that she did not intend to assault anyone, the proof being that she had not even nocked the arrow. Within seconds, she was out of the class and in the schoolyard, wandering around and thinking how unjust it was for them to misjudge her. Of course she would never shoot an arrow at anyone. How could they not know that?

Eva felt her new gym teacher did not like her as much as Mr. Coltman had the year before. Her suspicions were confirmed when she came to gym one day without her gym clothes. Eva had a good reason and thought her gym teacher, a woman, would understand. That morning, she realized it was gym day, but she also realized, to her dismay, that her legs were not shaved. She couldn't wear her shorts and expose her hairy legs. As she finished explaining her dilemma, whispering in her teacher's ear, the gym teacher mocked her with a heartless tone in front of everyone, stating it was no excuse. Eva was yet again suspended for the day.

As she walked toward the locker room, she saw some girls whispering and laughing while staring as she passed. Humiliated, and embarrassed, Eva left, her face as red as the skipping rope that lay on the gym floor.

Outside, Nolan was sitting on a bench enjoying the sunny day. He had decided not to attend his classes in order to enjoy the outdoors. Nolan had grown even more handsome than the year before. For a soon-to-be fifteen-year-old, he looked more like twenty. His physical features had gained him modeling contracts on occasion, and he hoped to be a star one day. His dream had won him first place in the mocking gallery, the other boys rejecting him increasingly as the days went by. Eva had enough mocking of her own to deal with. Therefore, hanging with Nolan was out of the question. She smiled at him, waved hello from afar, then walked on as if she had someplace to go. She hid in the cafeteria bathroom for the rest of gym class.

Eva didn't just feel victimized by her gym teacher. Geography class was painful too. Throughout the year, she sensed her geography teacher did not like her. She was impatient, her tone was condescending at times, and she treated Eva like a child. Eva had had enough of such treatment at home and did not appreciate being disrespected.

In early spring, Eva decided to create a crossword from scratch. She had a theme and had managed to create one that included over thirty words. She was proud of herself. She thought she would win an award for creativity and ingenuity, not that anyone had suggested there was any competition or reward anywhere.

In an attempt to have her masterpiece printed in the school newspaper as a year-end gift to all the students, Eva asked permission from her geography teacher, who was in charge of the school paper. She agreed to print the puzzle, to Eva's joy. However, Eva was devastated when she looked for her work of art in the last paper of the school year, only to realize it had not been added. Though enraged, Eva repressed her anger. A teacher who said "yes" to her face and "no" behind her back was capable of anything. Final exams were days away, and Eva did not want to be flunked out of spite by someone who had all the power over her geography grades.

She also had a morals and ethics class. Dr. Plummer entertained concepts considered to be avant-garde. Eva viewed his teachings as shocking and offensive. Dr. Plummer took delight in destroying any religious beliefs and mocked those who tried to defend them. He bragged that he was part of an elite group of an intelligent few. To be a member of this exclusive association, one had to have an IQ of at least 200. It was as if Dr. Plummer considered anyone who did not have his IQ as inferior. Most times, he talked down at the students. He constantly crushed arguments made by his students that did not align with his views.

During one class, Dr. Plummer proudly presented his doctoral study of personality traits. His theory showed that one could predict an individual's personality through his or her anatomic design. After an elaborate explanation of his theory, he proceeded to prove it by having every student fill out a thorough questionnaire. Once the answers were compiled, he would provide the results.

As promised, he gave the students their results the following week. Most students' physical attributes matched their personality traits, exactly like his doctoral study predicted. However, for some students, they did not match at all. In fact, their personality traits were the opposite of their supposedly matching anatomy.

Mark and Lewis were two of the few whose results clashed with the theory. They made it known to the class, declaring Dr. Plummer's theory did not work and that his doctoral study was a sham. This time, for once, the students were mocking the teacher.

Insulted, Dr. Plummer declared in a demeaning tone that the boys were simply too immature to have answered the questionnaire properly. He declared their test results null and void. As the students exited the classroom at the end of the day, many agreed that the thesis was flawed, but their teacher was too proud to admit it.

During one recess, Eva was experiencing her monthly period and needed to go change in the bathroom. When she came out of the stall, she realized, to her horror, that the garbage bin didn't have a lid, and anything in it would be visible to everyone. Embarrassed by what she had carefully wrapped in toilet paper, she chose to discreetly keep it in her purse, waiting for the end of recess when all the girls would be back in class before dropping her waste where it belonged.

Back at the bench where Nolan and a few other new friends were sitting, she sat quietly, waiting for the bell. The conversation having come to a standstill, Nolan grabbed Eva's purse, laughingly alluding to the fact that he wanted to look inside and see what was inside a girl's purse. Eva's face turned from white to red to green. She tried to grab it back, to no avail. The more she pleaded, the more he laughed, thinking it was funnier by the minute. Finally, the bell rang. Understanding that they had to get to class, he returned the purse to Eva, who sighed in relief. She swore never to risk such humiliation over the embarrassment of other girls seeing her throw away a soiled sanitary pad. She swore never again to sit with Nolan and his friends.

The school year passed without a boyfriend for Eva. Two weeks before summer holidays, she was standing on her tiptoes on the bottom of her metal locker. She was trying to reach the back of the upper shelf to grab a small yet important piece of paper stuck between the back wall and the shelf. Her posture extended her bum out and away from the locker. Lewis, who had become the most popular guy in school, happened to walk by Eva's locker at that moment. Throughout the school year, he had always had a girlfriend at his side, each one prettier and sexier than the previous one. This time he was alone and, seizing the opportunity, he slapped Eva's bum on his way past. Eva turned around, surprised and shocked. If looks could kill, he would have dropped dead. He walked away with a smirk.

You should not have looked at him that way, she thought. *That was social suicide. Now your chances of getting a boyfriend are lower than ever. You should have laughed at it and smiled as if you liked it.* But it was too late. She had done the unpardonable. Now Lewis was going to tell all his buddies that Eva was stiff and old fashioned. Her chances of getting a boyfriend were slimmer than ever now. Never mind being part of the cool gang after that.

At the last bell on the final day of grade eight, all the students exited their classes. Everyone was screaming with joy. Some ran toward the school buses. Others walked while throwing papers in the air, littering their path on the way home.

As she rushed toward her bus in the hysteria of the moment, Eva blurted out to Edith, in response to her question, that once she become an adult, she would like to travel the world as a nun to help people.

Edith stopped in her tracks and exploded in laughter. "Eva wants to become a nun!" she screamed. Everyone who heard laughed and mocked. However, in the frenzy of the moment, most students did not hear and continued to run toward their buses, as it was time to head home. The first bus driver closed his door, and the other drivers followed suit. Motors started, and all the buses left the school premises.

That was the end of it. Next year would be different, Eva hoped. She would find her prince, and all would be well. No one would remember the stupid things she had done and said. She would become popular and make plenty of new friends. Yet, in the depth of her being, she sensed her hopes were weakening in a free-fall spiral. The more she tried, the more she failed at being cool and important or fitting in. What was she going to do?

4

PARTY WITH ALCOHOL

This time she was awake. The alarm clock on her bedside table showed 4:00 p.m. The feeling of heaviness in her body had subsided, and her heart had resumed its normal cadence. Slowly getting out of bed, she went to the sparsely furnished kitchen. The decor coordinated with her bedroom: empty white walls and cheap used furniture. She welcomed the strong coffee aroma. A bowl of cereal would serve as breakfast, lunch, and dinner. She sat there gazing at the empty wall, rehearsing her past in her mind while her cereal lost its crunch, transforming into a soggy paste. Each memory seemed so far away that it was as if she was recalling someone else's life, the life of someone she wasn't sure she liked. The more she thought about it, the more she hated what she had become.

Why had it been so important to be popular and fit it? Why had she never felt good enough to be herself? Why had she gotten onto that slippery slope of needing a boyfriend so badly that her life degenerated to a point of affecting what she said and did, turning her into someone she was not? *Who am I truly?* she asked herself. *Who is Eva Day Rush?*

As Eva pondered these questions, she realized she had no answer. She had been living her life based on something she did not understand. Suddenly, she surprised herself by yelling, "Who cares if you have a boyfriend or not? Who cares if you're popular or not?"

Who cares? she thought. I care! she replied. But why? Hopelessness lurked in her heart as a voice in her mind replied: *Without a boyfriend, you're nothing.*

Her mouth was dry. She wished she had something to put in her coffee to spike it up. It would ease the pain in her chest. Lost again in her thoughts, her old diaries came to her mind. She knew she had kept them through her moves.

She headed back to her bedroom to search her closet. A plastic box fell on her head as she opened the door. The closet was filled with everything and anything. After preventing the contents of the top shelf from falling on her, pushing scarves, mittens, and wool shirts farther in, she took out several black garbage bags full of clothes. Once the bags were out of the way, she saw some small cardboard boxes piled on the floor amongst her shoes, belts, and purses. Reaching down, she pulled one out and hesitantly opened the box entitled "Grade 9." She started to read.

"October 12, Halloween is fast approaching, and so far, the school year has been without incident."

Eva stopped reading and closed the book with a loud clap while closing her eyes. She dreaded what had been written from her own hand years before. She remembered too well what had happened that day. With her eyes closed, she saw the events unfold in her mind. It was like being there all over again.

She had left her last morning class a few minutes before the end, having created an excuse to leave early. She was heading toward the cafeteria in the hopes of saving two seats for her and Natasha at their usual meeting place.

As Eva increased her stride to beat the crowd, she heard an unfamiliar voice. "Well, if it isn't our nun!"

Eva's blood froze in her veins. She stopped. A girl she did not know was leaning against the wall, smiling at her. Eva's heart leaped in her chest as she glanced at her. The girl was overweight and muscular. She had blue eyeshadow, her lower eyelids were adorned with a black line, and a heavy coat of mascara thickened her eyelashes. Her red cheek powder and red lipstick were too bright to match her long blonde frizzy hair, which was spiked over her head while falling down at the back to her shoulders, all hanging by a generous layer of hair spray. Her tight jeans revealed her overgrown thighs.

"And you're a whore!" Eva said without thinking.

The girl jumped on Eva, and they started to fight, but the girl was much stronger and larger than Eva, and in seconds Eva was on her knees facing her. Mr. Coltman's karate classes were a blur of the past, and her lack of practice proved detrimental. She played the weak victim card.

"You come to me with hatred in your heart, but I choose to forgive you. You can hit me all you want. I will not fight back."

At that moment, Edith appeared. "Jenny, leave her alone!"

"You know that cow?" Jenny asked as she released Eva from her firm grip. No one else was in the hall, so, lacking an audience, Jenny did not mind letting her prey loose. Edith convinced Jenny that it was in her best interest not to get into trouble again. Eva understood from their short conversation that Jenny was an inch away from getting expelled.

Jenny stepped back. Pointing her finger at her in a threatening gesture she said to Eva, "Don't you dare call me that again."

The bell rang, and the other students, oblivious to what had just taken place, crowded the halls. Eva sheepishly thanked Edith and then joined the crowd. Filled with anger and shame, she no longer felt like going to the cafeteria. She went outside instead, wishing she had the guts to hitchhike anywhere except Myerbell.

Settling for the farthest corner of the schoolyard, she sat on a bench, still shaken by what had just happened. *If this monster Jenny knows about what I said last year to Edith, what am I going to do if the word goes around? What if anyone also finds out about my secret? I shouldn't have said I wanted to be a nun! I'll deny it if anyone asks.*

She was suddenly distracted by a procession of four girls exiting the school grounds. Eva discreetly examined the girls as they passed in front of her. Oblivious to her presence, a tall skinny girl seemed to be the leader of the quartet. The other three followed her like breastfeeding puppies following their mother. She had seen this procession before; it seemed like a daily ritual. Every day at lunch, they would head two blocks down the road to a candy shop. Taking the money her parents gave her for lunch, the tall girl spent it on candy. On their way back to school, she would share the contents of her bag with the others. Eva wondered if the three girls would stick around if their "cash cow" suddenly stopped providing them with goodies. Eva certainly was not going to be one of those girls. However, she had to admit that the girl with the money was popular. She was buying it, but at least she had groupies.

Her thoughts were brought back to the event she had just experienced as she compared her lot with that of the tall girl. *I wish I had money to shut up anyone who tries to mock me. And how did Jenny find out what I said to Edith last year? Did she hear when Edith laughed out loud? She must have, unless Edith had been yapping about it recently.* Eva decided she was going to have a serious conversation with Edith, but not that day. She was too shaken to speak to anyone, even to Natasha.

"Natasha!" she exclaimed. *She must be looking for me everywhere,* she thought. Forgetting her vow of silence, she sprang up and headed toward the cafeteria.

Walking back to her kitchen with a box of journals in her arms, Eva despised herself. How cowardly she had been when facing Jenny, who never brought up that event again. It was in both girls' interest to forget it had happened. Even Edith had been silent about it. Tossing aside what was now an inedible bowl of mush, she made space for the box of journals. She took out a black plastic garbage bag. She was ready to throw away her past. But then she hesitated for a moment and opened a random page of another book. Staring at the journal entries, she remembered her grade ten and eleven years oh so well! A few people had mocked her, but Eva had managed over time to ensure that everyone who knew her got the message that she wanted to pursue a career as a psychologist and nothing else. She realized how much she needed to understand something about herself that still wasn't clear to her even now that she was in her early twenties. What happened? Why did her heart feel so empty and void?

In an attempt to find answers, she changed her mind and postponed her cleaning spree. Dropping the empty garbage bag on the floor, she read the entry entitled "November 16".

Five minutes were left before the buses would leave the school grounds. Danny's locker was right next to Eva's, and he was as late as her. Checking to ensure that everyone around them had left, she boldly asked him if he liked her. Danny froze in discomfort. She went on to say that she found him attractive and handsome and would like to get more serious with him. He replied that he didn't look at her that way and that he would rather stay friends. He mumbled about needing to rush to his bus and left in such a hurry that Eva almost felt the wind of his exit blow through her hair. The pang of emotional turmoil weighed heavily on her heart. The empty hole inside was growing larger and deeper. Agony turned to anger.

Eva was furious, hating herself for having had the nerve to tell Danny how she felt. Of course, he would say that. Guys liked to be in control and preferred to be the ones doing the wooing. She realized that even though they were entering the 1980s, boys were still boys. She hated to wait for them. And what was wrong with her, after all? Why did no boy desire her?

One time a guy told her of his affection for her. Bobby wanted to go out with Eva, for their platonic relationship to be more serious. Eva's hesitation toward him stemmed from the fact that Bobby smoked weed, and she hadn't even tried cigarettes. Bobby scared her. His long hair, potbelly, and 1960s look made Eva feel like he was a twenty-five-year-old who had never graduated from high school.

After Danny's brush-off that night, Eva's self-talk grew worse. She called Edith to vent.

"You need to relax!" Edith said after Eva had shared her ordeal. Her voice was different than usual, and Eva asked her if she was all right. Edith avoided the question, saying only that Eva needed to come to her place sometime. Edith declared that she possessed the secret to obtaining peace through a perfectly relaxing activity.

Sure enough, the following weekend Eva was at Edith's place—with her parents' approval, of course. She lied to them, pretending a science project was involved. Edith was alone at home the entire weekend, and the girls took advantage of it.

On Friday night, Eva had her first drink. She loved the tingling in her body but especially how the alcohol relaxed her to the point of being carefree. The loathsome hole in her heart shrank as she drank. She had a second drink and a third. As she became more intoxicated, it seemed as if the hole disappeared. Eva longed for that state of being to continue. As the alcohol did its job, she felt great.

Edith's mom had a full bar in the basement, and the girls drank and ate popcorn and chips while watching horror movies on TV. Eva drank to the point of blackout.

The next day, she woke up with her head a little foggy, but she was ready to repeat the experience. For fear of reprisal, Edith did not want her mom to notice the missing booze, so they reluctantly decided not to engage again into their new-found medicine—for that weekend at least.

At school Eva noticed how Mark was spending more time than ever on his skateboard and showed a particular interest in teaching her the skill. As the only girl around who was able to use a skateboard properly without embarrassing herself, Eva got some attention, which she relished. Playing the mystically magical new board game of elves, gnomes, half-orcs, and dwarves also made Mark enamoured with Eva. She was the only girl he knew at Myerbell High who wanted to engage in that special world of make believe.

Lewis, on the other hand, was also progressively attracting Eva. That year they shared French Literature class. Eva's mother was French, so Eva was fluent and found the class boring. That is, until she was caught cheating on an exam. She did not cheat out of fear of failure. She cheated out of wanting to get it over with quickly so she could be released from class early. This time, there was no threat of a twenty-four-hour suspension. Her French teacher affirmed in front of the entire class that Eva would fail. French Literature was a mandatory credit to graduate, so it would force her to stay behind one more year. Eva was devastated and humiliated. She could have taught the class herself, considering her knowledge of French.

After a visit to the principal's office and a few solemn promises, Eva was assured that because of all her excellent previous grades in the class, she would not fail the year—providing she did not cheat again.

The incident caught Lewis's attention. He hailed her on their way out of school that afternoon and invited her to his sixteenth birthday party. His parents were going to leave him home alone for the evening, and he promised it would be all fun and games. She accepted without hesitation.

Once Lewis was out of sight, she let out a discreet, "Yes!" It would be a great night, and maybe, just maybe, she would have her chance with Lewis.

To say Lewis lived in a house was an understatement. It was a mansion. Some would even call it a castle. Loud music filled the air, and Eva heard the drumbeat getting louder as she approached the front door. In the entrance hall was a big sign that said, "Happy Birthday, Lewis!" A movie had already started in the TV room, and couples lying in the dark were engaging in something other than watching a VHS release of the latest blockbuster.

There were more bedrooms than needed, and their indoor pool had all the paraphernalia of a public pool. Some guests were swimming in their underpants, others in their birthday suits. Everyone was having a lot of fun, and no one seemed to mind what anyone was wearing—or not wearing, for that matter.

The private gym adjacent to the pool had all the necessary equipment for bodybuilding, and a big mirror covered the wall dividing the two vast rooms. Both living rooms had been prepared to welcome several people, bowls of popcorn and chips as well as other snacks readily available on each table. The TV room was also stocked with goodies.

Eva chose to sit with Mark and Natasha in one of the living rooms on a comfortable and rather large rattan loveseat covered with comfy, festive cushions. It was the birthday room, where Lewis's birthday cake sat on the table as the official centrepiece. The cake was in three parts, each representing a football field in commemoration of his latest sports achievements. The biggest piece was three-layered with little plastic football players, a small chocolate football, white end-zone lines made of icing sugar, and two custom-made pretzels in the shape of football goal posts, one at each end. The other two pieces on each side represented a chocolate and candy crowd cheering on their team. Several people assembled in a circle around the table and looked at the cake in amazement. A couple of Lewis's friends had cameras and took pictures.

Eva and Natasha were not quite as comfortable as the rest of the joyous troop, and Mark noticed it. He went to the bar and brought them a glass of punch. He also brought George and introduced him to Natasha. George was slim and tall. His medium-length, light-brown hair was combed to the side and hid part of his face. His green eyes were striking. He invited Natasha to come and take a closer look at the cake and engaged in conversation with her.

Eva welcomed the drink and did not mind getting the loveseat exclusively for the two of them. Drinking alcohol at a party made her feel cool. The experience was different from the other times she drank. Her first experience with Edith had been fun, and the effect of alcohol was pleasant while it lasted. After her experience at Edith's, she had started drinking her parents' alcohol in secret, hoping they wouldn't notice. Drinking at Lewis's place made her feel like she was part of the gang, part of the fun. It erased all traces of stiffness. No one would consider her old fashioned now. The hole in her heart disappeared once again like magic—the magic of alcohol.

As the evening moved onward, they drank more punch. Mark was sitting close, his arm around her shoulders. He looked her in the eyes and moved his head toward her lips. They shared a long, passionate kiss. Mark had been waiting for so long for this that he got carried away. As they kissed, his hands furtively shifted from her shoulders to where Eva had not given permission. She froze and then began to relax again. The effects of the alcohol numbed her. She didn't resist the fondling.

"Ahem!" Natasha said. "My brother is here to bring us home. Are you coming?"

Mark and Eva smiled at each other, kissed one last time, and as previously agreed, Eva returned to Natasha's home to enjoy the rest of the weekend. She could not keep from smiling, and her entire body was tingling with delight and euphoria. She had kissed a guy who was part of the cool gang, and she was on Cloud Nine.

On Saturday morning, the two girls could not stop talking about how fun the party had been and how they could not wait to get back to school.

That evening, Natasha's brother, who was three years older than her, offered them each a cigarette. On the eve of Natasha's sixteenth birthday, both girls did not hesitate to indulge. The trio smoked together and enjoyed each other's company. Eva got a high from inhaling the smoke. She liked the dizzy feeling. Both girls giggled.

"Boy, if you get a buzz from a normal cigarette, what would it be like if it was weed?" Edith's brother asked. The girls giggled even more. But the statement resonated in Eva's mind. *If you get a buzz from a cigarette . . . imagine weed. . . .*

Eva did not talk about the discomfort she experienced when Mark touched her at the party. She wanted to fit in so much that she brushed off the feeling, focusing on how much fun the party was. She had known Mark long enough to believe he was a good guy and did not mean any harm. She also forgot that before entering the house, Lewis was the one she had wanted to be with. That thought did not even cross her mind.

Monday morning came, and the thought of going to school was nerve-wracking. What would Mark say to her? She began to worry. Had he been serious on Friday night? Were they now officially going out?

5

HALLOWEEN, FORTUNE-
TELLER, AND WEED

Lewis's gang hung around the large atrium entrance. It was the meeting place between classes and lunchtime. Sometimes the atrium entrance served as a take-off point for playing hooky. Eva had ten minutes before first class, so she headed straight there. Mark was waiting for her. He smiled as she approached. Then he took her in his arms and kissed her in front of everybody. She was ecstatic. It was official. She was now part of the cool gang.

Mark was gentle with Eva, and she loved the attention he gave her. Now she could hang around at the atrium entrance with the rest of the coolest gang at Myerbell. Lewis was usually there with Mark, George, and the other boys. The boys' girlfriends were automatically included in the gang. Natasha and Eva fit right in. Lewis had yet another girlfriend. Edith kept making advances to him, hoping his current relationship would not last, just like his previous relationships. Edith was determined to get him, as she had been secretly enamoured with Lewis since grade eight.

That summer, Mark kept in contact with Eva, and they met on occasion. Eva was glad that one of the boys from the cool gang found her attractive enough to make her his girlfriend. That was enough for her to forget Lewis. She rationalized that Lewis was out of her league. She liked Mark a lot and found him attractive.

The time they spent together slowly became more intimate, the fondling turning into activities that Eva did not challenge. She preferred to go along rather than risk the relationship. Now that she was seventeen, owned a driver's license, and could move around town easily, she considered herself adult enough to make her own decisions. She ignored the warning signs. It was like an inner signal trying to caution her. She pushed the alarm down so deep that she killed it. She had enough of her father telling her everything was dangerous and wrong. She certainly was not going to have an "inner bell" cautioning her needlessly.

Eva had not shared her inner turmoil with Mark. She thought she could manage it on her own. She did not want to be a bother to him. Besides, Mark had other issues to deal with. His life situation was far less impressive than Lewis's.

Mark lived with his mother in an old apartment that needed repairs. His dad had passed away many years before, and being a single, lonely child made Mark long for a mate. His mother did not work. She collected a monthly government cheque that barely made ends meet. Whatever money he got from odd jobs was given to his mother for food. Since he did not have money for driving lessons, he did not have a license.

In the fall of their last high school year, Eva and Mark were closer than ever. Eva had had enough of a boring life.

Her secret had less and less impact. Wetting the bed was now occasional. Not a soul at school knew about it: not Edith, not Natasha, and definitely not Mark. She was growing older, and that meant she could dare more. She wanted excitement, adventure, and thrills. She wanted to try new things. She particularly wanted to forget what was going on at home. Smoking weed was increasingly tempting, and it was only a matter of time before she indulged in it.

The emptiness she felt inside was unbearable, and alcohol was not enough. The memory of Natasha's brother's comment about cigarettes and weed echoed stronger and louder every day. *Imagine weed . . . Imagine weed. . . .*

Eva dropped her journal on the table. Reading farther was pure torture. The agony and turmoil in her stomach was too much. It was as if she was living the pain all over again. It was nighttime again. Turning on the kitchen light to help her see better as she read had prevented her from noticing evening settle in. Eva needed to get some air.

She opened the kitchen window and took a deep breath. The smell of asphalt, gasoline, and the weird odours coming from her neighbour's open kitchen window coupled with the noise of the car horns, ambulance sirens, and people walking and talking was invasive to her. "No one ever goes to bed in this place," she murmured as she slammed the window back down and turned on the ceiling fan instead. Eva did not need to read her journal to remember her deteriorating relationship with her dad.

The more Eva became a woman, the less she felt loved by her dad. The more she discovered life, the less her father made sense. Eva's breathing increased, and her heart pounded in her chest as she remembered that evening.

Her negative self-talk was at work. It had not vanished with the fact that she had a boyfriend. Surprisingly, it grew worse. *Life's not worth it. You do everything wrong. Mark is nice to you because he doesn't know you still occasionally wet the bed. Your dad doesn't care. There's nothing you can do that is good enough for him. Life hurts too much. You would be better off dead.*

This time she was going to take a bigger and better knife. While her father was watching TV and her mother was folding clothes in the master bedroom, Eva snuck into the kitchen and grabbed a knife that would not cause superficial wounds. She went into her bedroom, determined to cut her wrist and bleed to death. She closed the door, sat on her bed, and began the process. Again, the blood dripping on her bedcover gave her nausea. She hid her bleeding wrist in her pillowcase and walked to the bathroom, which was at the opposite end of the house, to get the anti-nausea pills that would cause sleepiness while she bled out. Before she got there, Eva passed out in front of the bathroom door. Her mother heard the fall and found her lying in the doorway, blood from her wrist leaking through the pillowcase.

Eva's mother nursed her out of her fainting spell and brought her back to her room. After many tears and explanations, a plan of action was agreed upon.

Later that week, Eva was at the psychologist's office. She sat down and was not too sure what to say. She was not even sure what was going on inside. How could some stranger expect her to voice it? Each week, she attended a one-hour session, and each week, she talked about what was going on at school and at home with her parents, especially her father. After about three months, Eva began to consider the sessions a waste of her time. She was disappointed, as her expectations were unmet.

She had hoped the psychologist would have given her some magic formula to make the hole inside her disappear for good. She had hoped he would tell her how to fix her relationship with her father, and she would have liked him to tell her what to do or say to silence the negative voice in her head. But he did none of the above.

Eva convinced her mother and therapist that she was better and that she no longer felt the need for therapy. She certainly did not mention her disappointment with the process. She simply ignored the inner alarm by muffling it with occasional drinks.

No one at school knew she was seeing a psychologist, and Eva was not about to tell anyone. It was embarrassing. She was determined to keep it a secret, the same way she had kept her other secret. She had failed to end her miserable life. She considered herself a failure, but didn't want anyone to know. She was trying so desperately to fit in and had been longing for it for so long. Now she was making even stronger efforts to hide her pain.

One morning after yet another argument with her dad, she walked to the atrium entrance at a determined pace. Today would be the day she would smoke weed.

She met with Edith and spilled her guts. "My dad never understands me. He's so old fashioned and mean. He thinks everything is dangerous, and I can't stand it anymore!"

Edith, who had previously managed to get stuff from Bobby in the hopes of sharing it with Lewis, offered it to Eva instead. Lewis's new girlfriend was hanging on to the relationship longer than Edith had expected. The two girls disappeared into a corner of the schoolyard, away from prying eyes, and lit up.

This time, Eva not only felt relaxed, she also felt high-spirited. It was a new feeling that she enjoyed even more. The magical weed not only erased the hole, it replaced it with giggles.

When Edith and Eva returned to the atrium entrance, Natasha, George, and Mark were waiting for them. Mark took Eva in his arms. "Next time invite me in," he whispered. He looked into her eyes and waited for her response. Eva replied with a giggle and a nod.

Natasha smiled at the girls. "Can I tell them?" she asked. Edith was too gleeful to object. "Guess where we've all been invited this weekend?" Natasha asked.

For Halloween that year, Edith had decided it would be fun to have a séance and tarot card reading. She had organized a private party at her house, and the highlight of the evening would be a fortune teller.

That Saturday night, Eva and Natasha found it odd that, as they walked toward the sidewalk entrance of the house, no inside lights were lit. Thinking they were too early, they checked the time, only to realize they were ten minutes late. They rang the doorbell. As the door opened, it screeched with a cryptic sound, giving them the shivers. Dressed in black, Edith ushered them inside. "Take your shoes off and come sit with the others," she whispered. "Mark and George are already here."

Edith brought them to the living room. All the lights were off, and it took a few minutes for the girls to get used to the dark. It was a decent-sized room. Nine other people sat on the shag carpet in a circle around a low oval table that had eleven small, narrow candles on it, which also formed a circle. The rest of the furniture had been moved against the wall to maximize the limited space. Through the dim light of the lit candles, the girls spotted their sweethearts. Natasha sat next to George. As Eva moved to sit between Mark and Natasha, she recognized some other faces from school, although she did not know their names.

Two guys sat to Mark's left. The guy closest to him had a black Mohawk. On his neck was a dog collar with metal spikes. His eyes had thick black lines around them, similar to Jenny's eyes. His ears were pierced with what looked like half-inch-thick black plastic nails. The other guy's hair was bright red, and his face was covered with acne. Next to him was a heavily overweight girl, but Eva could not see her face clearly. She could not see much of the others either.

The soft background music sounded like a mystical symphony of instruments that Eva could not recognize. The fortune teller passed around a few of what looked like hand-rolled cigarettes. One after the other, each person inhaled a puff and then handed the joint to the next person.

Mark took it first. Eva imitated him perfectly, and both smiled as they started to feel the effect. Their first time smoking weed together. Eva thought it was so intimate and reassuring to have Mark beside her. Smoking weed in Mark's arms in a dark living room was so much better than doing it in the schoolyard alone with Edith.

It was only when the fortune teller started to speak that Eva realized she was actually an older woman. With solemnity, she softly directed everyone to close their eyes, join hands, and listen to the music penetrate their body. Eva was captivated by the entire event.

After a short time listening, they opened their eyes and released each other's hands. The fortune teller ceremoniously picked up tarot cards from a colourful handmade pouch and began to read the future, addressing each person present. The candlelight revealed the images on the cards, but it was hard to see the fortune teller's features.

Siting with her legs crossed on a carpet was not a familiar position for Eva. She noticed that a few others had changed position to be more comfortable. Some had taken couch cushions and used them for comfort. Others had their legs stretched out. As time went on, more weed was passed around. Then the second part of the evening began.

Once the fortune telling was done, the lady stopped the music and asked everyone to close their eyes, join hands, and be still. She was more ceremonious than ever as she started making ritualistic noises in her throat. She encouraged everyone to imitate her. The incantations lasted long enough for Eva to notice. However, the effect of the drugs suppressed any thought of speaking up. The attempts to make the dead speak increased in speed and vigour. But after all the conjuring was said and done, no dead person spoke.

The fortune teller closed her séance with another incantation and then slipped out of the house, leaving everyone lying on the carpet. Most of them, including Eva, had fallen asleep.

When she woke up, it was 3:00 a.m. She realized in a panic that she needed to get home. As she tried to gently release herself from Mark's arms, he woke up and asked if she was OK. Natasha and George were sleeping too. Eva had to wake up Natasha, so she could take her home, which inevitably woke George. Eva did not feel very good and wondered if she would be able to drive. She concluded she would be all right, since she had not had anything to drink. They hugged Edith and whispered good night as the four of them tiptoed out of the house.

It was raining outside. They did not linger long. George had his own car and drove Mark home. Eva dropped off Natasha on her way home.

Alone in the car, Eva realized to her disappointment that she no longer felt relaxed, as the weed's effect was subsiding. Frustration was rebuilding and her inner alarm tried to surface, as if the fortune teller's incantation was suddenly working on her. It was trying to speak to her. She felt unsettled, and internal turmoil was quickly building up. In an effort to avoid negative self-talk, she rationalized about how she felt relaxed when smoking. The rationalization and fatigue won out. Her inner alarm was silenced once again.

Months passed. January came, and graduation ceremony preparations were underway. The school drama teacher was leading the project.

Mr. Muller was fun to be with, partly because drama class was fun in and of itself but also because Mr. Muller knew how to speak to seventeen-year-olds. The graduate class felt respected by him, because he could relate to them.

He was a short, plump man with a black moustache. His hair looked like the barber had placed a bowl on his head and cut around it. However, the curling ends gave it an unevenness that made his look simple and pleasant. He had a way of making students laugh, and the various short theatrical presentations they did throughout the year were interesting. They stimulated their eager minds and, interestingly enough, instilled in them a passion for old and modern literature alike.

The patchy group that formed on the first Wednesday meeting could never have been predicted by anyone, not even Edith's famous fortune teller.

Jimmy wanted to organize a science fair. Nolan wanted to organize a fashion show. Both had a common goal to raise funds to reduce the graduation ball entrance fees. The costs included the professional disc jockey fees, the hall rental, and the purchase of snacks and beverages for the evening, and it all amounted to a lofty sum. Jenny wanted to ensure the graduation night included certain musical styles and volunteered herself as the one who would select which disc jockey was hired. Bobby wanted to ensure the least possible number of adults in the hall and volunteered to determine which teachers would be invited. He suggested others could become science fair judges.

At first, they argued about what type of evening it would be, formal or casual. They decided both would be approved. Eva already had her dress in mind.

While Jimmy connected with a few others to organize the science fair, it was determined that Nolan, Henrick, and George would model the guys' clothes. Edith, Eva, and another girl would model the girls' clothes.

Henrick had undergone a metamorphosis over their high school years. He no longer had buckteeth. He had worn braces for several years and also had surgery. He'd turned out to be handsome and Eva was glad for him. Nolan and Henrick were best friends. They were always together. Natasha was going to help with everything behind the scenes, and Mark agreed to help her with that.

Their time was spent organizing the fashion show notwithstanding, everyone still needed to attend class. Eva divided her time between studying and making the necessary preparations. Her grades were good, and she knew she would graduate. She never doubted it, except for the day when she cheated in French class.

While she was so occupied, she did not feel the pain of the big hole inside. She took Mark's affection as compensation for her lack of self-esteem. She smoked, drank, or did both, bringing about a false sense of the peace and calm she craved. Turmoil, frustration, and anger always reared up like an unwelcome virus. Each time she felt the effect of the substances dwindle, the craving for her next fix grew stronger.

6

GRADUATION NIGHT

That winter, in a desperate attempt to regain her daughter's relationship, Eva's mother brought her to a gathering of some kind. Her mother's friend greeted them at the door. She addressed Eva with polite words, then engaged in an unsolicited conversation about the state of her spiritual life. Eva assured her mother's friend that she was doing well spiritually and then, as politely as possible, ended the conversation by agreeing to whatever she was saying, even though she did not understand a word of it. "Do you have the light in your eyes? Have you received the fire?" *What on earth does she mean by that?* Eva wondered while answering yes to both questions.

Another night, she attended a meeting where her father was giving—as the leader of the meeting called it—his "testimony." Her father shared how he had started drinking, why he drank, and how and why he had stopped drinking alcohol. Eva was teary and felt a gentle yet cautious rekindling of affection toward him.

After his testimony, several adults came to talk with her, asking how her life was and declaring that she would also benefit from attending such meetings. Eva reassured each member of her small audience that her life was perfectly fine and that she did not need meetings at all. *They obviously don't know me,* she thought.

She went on to say that she was in the process of graduating from high school, working hard at graduation preparation. She had a boyfriend who loved her dearly and had many good friends. Everything in her life was perfect. She was glad her father had found something positive for his life, but it was not for her.

What's wrong with them? Eva wondered as she sipped her tasteless orange juice, pretending to listen to the ongoing conversation. *Can't they see how joyful and fulfilled I am with my life right now? Isn't my happiness evident? These old people are blind and know nothing. They just don't know how to have good fun.*

Back at school, during lunchtime, Eva felt the need for a yoga pause and decided to enjoy a time of meditation in the quietest room at school. She had been doing yoga at a private gym one evening a week and had enjoyed how easy it was for her. All her classmates were mature women who did not have her flexibility. In an attempt to be respectful, she tried hard not to let on how funny they looked when attempting various positions.

Eva found Mr. Brown, who was in charge of the school chapel, and asked permission to go to the chapel to pray. Perceiving her attempt to deceive him, he looked her straight in the eyes. "Are you truly going to pray? You're not going to do any funny business in there, are you?"

Eva assured him in a purposeful tone that she was determined to pray in the chapel and wanted the quietness of the room. He agreed she could go, reiterating that he trusted she was going to do what she'd said. Eva exited the room triumphantly, convinced she had sold him one. *Am I a good actress or what?*

As she entered, she immediately felt something peaceful outside of her, something in the room. She locked the door behind her and shut the blinds. Her heart pounded in her chest. She could not understand why, since she felt such peace surrounding her.

She stood up, facing the little altar in front of religious artifacts with which she was all too familiar. She had seen such sacred objects many times before and knew their significance. Brushing off the guilt, she engaged in the first step of the famous yoga pose Surya Namaskar—or sun salutation. No sooner had she joined her hands together than she heard a voice of authority in her heart. *Get out of here, you deceiver! You will not mock me!*

Freaked out, Eva ran out of the chapel in a panic and told no one. She certainly was not going to tell Mr. Brown, and she had even less motivation to tell anyone else, because they would think she was going crazy.

To celebrate Edith's eighteenth birthday, Bobby agreed to host a party in his unfinished basement. The cement floor was cold, and the walls, isolated with foam sheets, still revealed the two-by-fours. But no one cared. It was fun to have one big room in which to dance and laugh, and the old sofas and cushions on the floor were fine to sit on. Edith invited everyone she knew. Eva recognized some faces but also noticed some other friends who were much older than the people she knew.

Alcohol was flowing, but weed and other substances were in greater abundance. Edith tried something Eva wouldn't dare out of fear. Mark didn't like it either.

Finally, Bobby stood up and addressed the crowd. "And now, I will hypnotize my disciple. Observe in amazement what the Great Bobby can do!"

Eva had always been uncomfortable with Bobby. That night she feared him more than ever. She was glad Mark was with her and did not have a good feeling about the entire charade.

Edith was severely drugged, and it was evident that Bobby had her at the tip of his fingers. He told her to bend forward and then backward. His third command was for her to hold her breath while manoeuvring her hands and elbows in a particular way. His last command was a shout. "Let go!" Edith fell on the cement floor, convulsing vigorously.

Everyone was fascinated by the "show" and cheered and applauded as Edith got up without a scratch but also without any memory of anything she had done. Eva was frightened and told Mark she wanted to go home.

As they tried to leave quietly, Edith ran toward them all lovey-dovey, wanting to hug them both. She grabbed Mark and kissed him on the mouth right in front of Eva. Without waiting for any reaction, she turned toward Eva and also kissed her on the mouth. Her eyes were bloodshot. Eva knew it was not time to talk to her. As they left, they heard the crowd cheering and applauding for something they did not care to inquire about.

Now she understood why George and Natasha had declined the invitation to attend the party. Eva agreed with Mark that this type of party was too hardcore for them.

They were just into weed and alcohol, and they considered it innocent fun.

Eva dropped Mark at his place and then headed home. The light snowfall was increasingly degrading the road conditions. It was as if the night was darker than usual. Headlights and streetlights were flashing in her eyes. Eva could not see well, and her inexperience as a driver made her nervous. She was following the car in front of her too closely, and when she saw the red brake lights, it was too late.

The impact shook her. A lady came out of the car Eva had just hit. Bending toward the driver's window, she asked if Eva was OK. Eva affirmed that she was. They agreed that the proper procedure was to call the police. They pulled their cars off the road and entered a nearby restaurant.

While waiting for the police, Eva went to the phone booth to call her parents. It was their car, and she needed to inform them of the accident. She was apprehensive of her father's reaction. Having damaged the front bumper, she thought, *He's going to kill me.*

Her mother answered the phone. From her tone of voice, Eva could tell she had woken them up. Perplexed by the lateness of the call, her mother asked if Eva was OK. After sheepishly reassuring her of her welfare, Eva explained that she had been in an accident. No sooner than she'd confirmed the car damages were minor did her father take the phone and ask the same question her mother just asked. "Are you OK? Darling, your welfare is all that matters. Come home with the car, and we'll have it repaired. It's just material. What matters is you."

Eva could not believe what she had just heard. She had not expected this reaction. She wondered what had happened to her father to be so nice to her in such a situation. Why didn't he yell at her for wrecking the car? Still in shock, she thanked him and promised to get home as soon as possible. She hung up as the police car pulled into the restaurant's parking lot.

Once all the necessary documents were filled out, Eva drove home to the sound of a harrowing engine and a crooked bumper. Although she did not get hurt physically, there was unrest in her heart from the experience at Bobby's place. With the car accident that followed, Eva would have loved a drink right there and then, but that would have to wait for another time.

Back at her kitchen table, Eva could still see the accident in her mind. She brushed off the negative thought and replaced it with the souvenirs of the event that followed shortly after. While pouring herself a coffee, which had just percolated, she reminisced about the glory days of the fashion show.

They had worked hard to find several sponsors and storeowners to be involved in the project. Several hundred people were in attendance in the school auditorium, including Eva's parents and Mark's mother. However, most of the crowd consisted of high school students. The master of ceremonies did a great job with presenting the clothes, and the music was well blended with the commentary.

To create an interlude halfway through the fashion show, Mark did a drum solo. Many cheered in enthusiasm for his talent. The clothes modeled were all part of the spring collection, and the grand finale was the bathing suits. Many whistled in admiration, although Eva wasn't sure if the whistles were for her bathing suit or her. She greatly enjoyed the attention, basking in the exhilaration that it provided.

A few weeks later, the science fair was held in that same auditorium. Eva and Natasha went to encourage Jimmy and his friends, who were presenting different science projects. Dr. Plummer was one of the judges. Eva thought she preferred him to be at the science fair than the graduation dance.

Twelve participants proudly exhibited their projects. Eva and Natasha found some interesting and complex and others less elaborate. One displayed a system of pulleys and blocks that, after pulling a string, made a motor start without the need for gas. Inside what seemed like a lead box, metallic marbles hit each other through some sort of rubber surface that created a never-ending force to activate the motor. At least that's what Eva understood from the explanation. Although she didn't understand it all, she was fascinated.

It came as no surprise when Jimmy announced, with a solemn voice, that this project had won first prize. Jimmy had agreed that since he was the head of the science fair, he would not participate in the contest. Eva and Natasha found it noble of him but could not help noticing how Jimmy was overly excited that the pulley project was the winner. Neither of them knew who the inventor was; it seemed like it was the first time they had seen him. Jimmy and the inventor looked alike and seemed like long-time friends. It was only some time later that Eva found out the winner was Jimmy's younger brother. *No wonder he won the prize! They must all be geniuses in his household*, Eva thought.

With Easter out of the way, a spring party was set for the last weekend of May. It was a friend of a friend's birthday party, where alcohol flowed, and drugs were easily accessible. Eva thought that because Mark was by her side, nothing bad would happen. Mark would keep her safe.

The next morning, she woke up at Mark's place, a blank in her memory. She could not remember what had happened the night before. All she recalled was the glass of wine she drank and Mark getting up to fetch more. That was the last image she had of the evening.

Vomit was everywhere on the floor of the bathroom, where she was lying. Mark saw she was awake. "I'm not cleaning this up," he said. "And you better clean it all before my mother sees this." Eva sensed impatience in his tone and did not like it. It was the first time Mark had spoken harshly to her. Something had happened at the party, but Mark would not tell her. He stated that if she didn't remember, it wasn't worth discussing.

The graduation party was only weeks away, and Mark's attitude toward Eva was increasingly awkward. But Mark said it was all in her head. Eva chose to silence her internal alarm bell, even though it was trying to alert her that something was actually wrong.

Eva stopped reading her journal and realized that, to this day, she still did not know what had happened at the party that made Mark change so drastically toward her. Natasha and George did not attend the party, and Edith had been too fried to remember anything. Eva didn't know the other people attending well enough to ask anyone. Staring at her cold coffee, she got up and threw it in the sink. She poured herself another cup of the black liquid while reflecting bitterly on the graduation night events.

Everything was as they had planned. Some had their best jeans on, some were in suits. Eva wore her handmade dress. With her mother's help, she had purchased material and sewed a nice dress from a wedding gown pattern. It was knee high, and the white material was of high quality, the type used for wedding gowns. The bust was made of delicate embroidery with two pink laces on the side. The long sleeves ended with fifteen small, hand-covered buttons and hand-threaded buttonholes that her mother had stitched. Eva saw the love in her workmanship and was touched that her mother would take such care and attention toward her. The gown had been finished for months. It had everything a wedding gown should have, except of course the traditional veil. That would have been too obvious. Secretly, Eva considered her graduation party like her wedding with Mark. However, she did not tell a soul for fear of being mocked.

That night, everyone was at the hall. The music was varied to please all styles, and to Eva's surprise, Jenny had made a good choice of disk jockey. The winning science fair projects were on display on a table near the entrance with the names of the proud winners. On the wall were framed pictures and a collage of photos of the fashion show, which had raised a lofty sum. Everyone involved was proud of the projects' success.

Many people were on the dance floor. Some were talking at tables, and others were outside smoking. It was a beautiful evening, the nice June weather promising a hot summer.

As conversations unfolded, it was exciting to hear everyone's future plans. Some had been accepted at Real Mountain University. Jimmy had obtained a full scholarship in science with a specialization in chemistry. He was one of the few who were accepted in a special program that combined a bachelor's degree and a doctorate. Jimmy was heading for eight years of full-time university research. Everyone cheered for him. Lewis laughed when he heard the news. "Better him than me."

Some had found employment in the big city, and some right in Myerbell. Mark was one of them. He was staying behind, having landed a position as a salesman for an insurance company that promised him the moon if he worked hard. Everyone was happy for each other, filled with hope and anticipation for the future. It was such a glorious beginning to the evening. Things could not be going better.

Then Mark announced he was ready to head home. Eva looked at him, shocked and disappointed. She had hoped to stay longer at the graduation dance. It was only ten o'clock.

She had warned her parents that she was not coming home, thinking she would be partying all night. Mark insisted on heading home and asked Eva to come with him. Despite her disappointment, she did not resist.

Throughout the winter and spring, she had developed a scenario in her mind as to what the evening would be like. She had fantasized about it for months. She would party with the gang until the middle of the night, and then she would head to Mark's place for the grand finale. Mark had pretty much the same fantasy, except for the part about partying all night with the gang. He had been thinking about going to his place as early as possible to enjoy time alone with Eva.

Because of the tension they had experienced in their relationship during the weeks prior to graduation, Eva judged it wise not to argue with Mark. She knew what he had in mind, as they had talked about it many times. The vague memories of her childhood girls' games were far in the past. Her naïve curiosity as to what men looked like had been quenched a long time ago. However, she had never gone all the way. Her time with Mark had always ended with foreplay. And so far, he had not insisted on anything more.

Still sitting at her kitchen table, Eva sobbed uncontrollably. She reached for the tissue box on the kitchen counter and blew her nose noisily. The more she remembered of that next morning, the more she sobbed, and the more tissues she used. She felt devastated. It was like she was there all over again.

That next morning, after she had given herself to him, she felt more in love than ever. She was expecting him to feel the same. Mark had been so nice to her all this time, she thought that whatever had happened a few weeks back could not have been bad enough to break up their relationship. But Eva could sense that Mark was not the same. He was even more distant than usual. She was crushed. They needed to talk, and the conversation could not wait.

7

LIFE IN THE BIG CITY

E va suggested a drive around town, to which Mark agreed half-heartedly. They drove around for a while. As Mark talked, he brought the conversation somewhere Eva did not want to go. "We had a good time in high school, didn't we? I enjoyed being with you, and I have great memories of what we had."

"Yes, high school was great," Eva replied as she drove along the wooded land separating the north side from the south. Traffic was light. "I'm not upset that it's over though. I can't wait to be gone from here and move to Real Mountain, where I'll be away from my parents, especially my father."

"I'm glad you feel that way, Eva. It'll be easier for both of us."

Eva stopped the car on the side of the road and looked straight at him. "What are you talking about?"

Mark explained how their lives had been different all along. He said they were not meant to be together, and that since he was starting full-time work and she was moving to the city to embark on a four-year university program, it would be best if they parted ways. Eva was in shock. She could not believe her ears.

Tears running down her face, she begged him to tell her what had happened at the May party that made him change so much and made him not want to be with her. He said it was not important and that she would have to figure things out on her own. This was the last time they would be together. "You're free now," he said. "Free to love whomever you wish."

Eva was too shaken to move. Tears blurred her vision, and her left shirtsleeve played the role of tissue, since she didn't have any in the car. Wiping her nose, she told Mark she still loved him and did not want their relationship to end.

"It's better that way," he insisted. She could see in his eyes that though his mouth was declaring words, his heart did not believe them. She asked if he still loved her. He turned away and stared at an empty space beyond a wheat field. "No," he said.

Eva sobbed even more. How could she have given herself only the night before to someone who no longer loved her? When did his love end? Why did he play along with the role of boyfriend? He had used her for his personal satisfaction. How could she have been so blind? Eva hated herself. Her sadness turned to anger. "Get out! Get out of my car. You can hitch-hike home. I don't care. Just leave!"

As she drove away, her tires screeched on the pavement. She wiped her tears and headed home.

Alone in the house, she sighed in relief that her parents were out, sparing her the ache of having to explain her red eyes and flustered face.

She took off her graduation dress in disgust and put on pyjamas for comfort. She needed to start packing. While pulling her personal things out of the wardrobe, she found a small religious artifact. She scoffed at it and reminisced about her religious upbringing. If a higher being existed, where was he now? Her pain was proof enough that God did not exist. If God were real, he would not allow her to experience such sorrow. Grabbing some empty boxes, she started putting her things in them.

The following weeks were busy for Eva. She was moving to the city and getting ready to enter university in the fall. University was the best excuse she had to justify her escape from her parents, especially her father. The excitement to move out almost made her forget the pain caused by her separation from Mark. She could not wait to leave Myerbell.

That July, Eva and Natasha planned to celebrate their eighteenth birthday at a popular bar in Real Mountain called the Zone Bar and Grill. It was a block away from the university's athletic fraternity and within walking distance for anyone who attended Real Mountain University. The restaurant was a sports bar with a TV screen on each wall. It broadcast sporting events, including games on game nights. It also had a small dance floor for in between games. The restaurant mostly attracted university students who needed to let off some steam from the stress of essays, reports, and exams.

That night, golf was on TV, but no one cared. They invited all their friends, and everyone from the Myerbell High atrium entrance gang came, except Mark. The recent break-up kept Mark at bay from everyone. His absence was palpable, but Eva chose to celebrate her coming of age with great pomp.

When the girls entered the bar, the gang was waiting for them at reserved tables. They greeted them with, "Surprise!" as if the girls did not know. They pretended to be surprised, and after the laughter died down, the drinks started to flow.

When it came time to head to her apartment, Lewis offered to escort Eva home, as she was in no condition to drive her newly acquired 1971 Pinto. Eva could hardly walk and needed to hold onto Lewis with every zigzagging step.

She passed out right in front of her door. Lewis took her shoes off, picked her up, brought her to her bed, and left her there all dressed up. Then he proceeded back to his fraternity house.

The next day, Eva had planned to go job hunting, but her hangover was brutal. She treated her condition with a good dose of caffeine, rendering the afternoon manageable. She loved the big city and being on her own was freeing. She kept her Pinto in her building's underground garage and reserved it exclusively for long-distance travelling. Eva bussed around the city, as parking was hard to find, and traffic was a nightmare. Finding a job would be easy, as Real Mountain was thriving.

Natasha had moved in with George and two other roommates in a bigger apartment. Lewis received a brand-new car for his eighteenth birthday and was living in a fraternity house on campus on a full football scholarship. As the rookie quarterback, he hoped that, within a few years, he would be recruited as a professional player.

August meant Frosh Week. Each department had its own rituals. Eva was not excited about being alone in an unfamiliar place with unfamiliar faces. It was different than the transition from NSE to Myerbell High. Different indeed.

Bobby, Edith, Natasha, and George had all been accepted in the arts department. Bobby was majoring in general art. Edith's major was theatre. Natasha and George were in design and fashion. Eva was enrolled in psychology.

Eva wished she was part of a sorority. It looked so wonderful in movies. But because she had been denied bursaries and grants, she had to fend for herself to pay her education fees and personal bills. Eva's parents did not have the money to help out. Therefore, a sorority was not an option. And in the psychology department, the girls' sororities were only for those who lived on campus. Living on campus was out of Eva's reach.

Frosh Week was quiet for Eva. She heard of several incidents that occurred though. One guy ended up in the hospital because of a hazing ritual. Most sorority and fraternity leaders in the mainstream programs practiced hazing. Bobby and Edith were some of the victims. Bobby had to dip naked three times in the polluted river that ran through Real Mountain. Edith had to eat live bugs and walk in her socks for the week.

Eva made do by sitting in the small café located next to her apartment. Outside the café were little tables and parasols, imitating a French bistro. However, the busyness and noise of the boulevard ruined the ambiance.

In the morning of the last day of Frosh Week, Eva was sitting alone at the café. She had started preparing for classes by reading mandatory psychology manuals. That day was particularly busy at the café, and all the chairs were taken, except for one facing Eva at her table. A good-looking guy approached and asked if he could sit with her. She smiled and nodded.

Returning to her reading, she did not notice him pulling a book out of his backpack. Realizing what she had in her hands, he laughed and held up his book. "We're reading the same textbook, *Psychology 101*, right?"

Eva looked at him carefully and for the first time realized how handsome he was. She smiled and asked if he was enrolled in psychology as well. He said he was, and they engaged in a pleasant conversation.

His name was Albert, and he had just moved into his apartment. They realized they were also neighbours and that Albert's apartment was two floors below Eva's. He had been born and raised in a small town a few hours away from Real Mountain in the opposite direction of Myerbell. Since he had just arrived in town the week before Frosh Week, he knew no one. Eva offered to show him around, adding she did not know much of the city herself, having arrived only a month before. She explained that she had also enrolled in a guided tour that familiarized students with the university's facilities. She suggested he come with her.

That afternoon, they both attended the tour and got to know each other better. Eva liked Albert, and it was obvious that he liked her.

After the traditional orientation week, classes started. The professors treated them as adults—which they were—and there was no leniency. Psychology being a restricted field, the university enrolled double the number of students in the first year and aimed to eliminate the weakest ones throughout each semester.

"Look around, everyone. Look now! Because by April next spring, half of you will not be here anymore. It's my job to make your life so miserable that only the toughest and strongest survive," their Psychology 101 teacher stated.

Eva shivered. Sitting next to her, Albert's demeanour reflected the same sentiments. She had not seen that coming and hadn't expected university to be so heartless.

When she went back to her apartment that night, she felt lonely. With Mark no longer in her life, she wanted to be with someone, talk with someone with whom she felt comfortable. But even more so, she felt the need to be held. She longed for affection. She remembered the night of her birthday party, when Lewis had been particularly attentive to her. All evening he had sat next to her while he placed his arm on top of her chair, just enough to surround her yet not touching her shoulders. She was also touched that he had not taken advantage of her that night. She wondered if Lewis was simply a good friend or if he thought of her as something more. His signals were unclear. Was he interested in her?

Remembering her fiasco with Danny years earlier, she was not going to open her heart to him, even though she knew he had no girlfriend at the moment. She was determined not to be the first one to talk. She called Lewis nonetheless, only to ask him out for a beer at the Zone. To Eva's surprise, he agreed. She made great efforts not to let him know she was surprised. She wanted to portray assurance, even though every atom of her being felt doubt.

The music was loud, but the ambience was stimulating. To Eva's relief, the two of them were the only ones from the gang who showed up that night. The Zone was the gang's hangout, so it was unusual that none of their friends were there. When she saw Lewis, she realized that, it had been him she'd wanted all along. She had brushed it off for over two years because of her relationship with Mark. She remembered how, on his sixteenth birthday, she had secretly wished that Lewis had sat beside her on that loveseat. She was burning to tell him. The more they talked about everything and anything, the more Eva wanted to tell him how she felt. Lewis had a nonchalant attitude, and she was never sure what he really thought. He always displayed assurance, and Eva's lack of it contrasted bitterly.

When Eva talked, Lewis seemed interested enough. She did not know what to think when Lewis told her that he no longer had a girlfriend and was as free as a bird. Since everyone knew that, why did he mention it? Was he saying it to tell her he liked being free and did not want to get involved with anyone? Or was he saying it to signal that he was interested in her? She didn't know for sure, but she was too embarrassed to ask him openly.

The evening ended when Lewis announced he had to go to bed early, since he had football practice the next morning. Eva interpreted it as a signal that she was boring him.

"Oh, of course," she said. "I understand. I have to study as well." The two friends went their separate ways.

Albert was in most of Eva's classes, and they usually sat next to each other. They also studied together in between classes, and most mornings, they had coffee together at the café where they first met.

Evenings at the Zone succeeded each other, with various members of the gang hanging out. Friday and Saturday nights were particularly popular. Bobby had what seemed like unlimited access to drugs and used the Zone to discreetly sell. Eva learned that he had friends who had access to a lot of things and that it was in her best interest not to question him.

Eva had been working as a security guard in a museum for a few months. Even though she worked in the evenings, she managed to get Friday and Saturday nights off. Attending classes during the day and working evenings from Sunday to Thursday was hard. Watching over artwork in a museum at night when no one was there was also boring. The job was easy and would have allowed plenty of time for study; however, she was not permitted to study or even read a book. She hated her job.

By then, Edith had forgotten all about Lewis and had started dating one of Bobby's friends. The guy was several years older than her and a member of a notorious motorcycle gang. Jenny was also a member.

During mid-semester, when projects were due, Edith had to make a report on various painters from the Renaissance era. It was Friday night, and the report was due on Monday at 10:00 a.m. Failure to hand it in at the beginning of class was an automatic zero.

Edith sat at a booth near the loudest speaker of the Zone and wrote fervently. Eva, who noticed her sitting alone, wondered why she was doing homework at a bar. She approached with two beers in hand. Edith politely declined.

"Are you OK?" Eva asked, surprised.

Edith smiled. "Of course. I took something to keep me awake and alert. My brain is so clear right now, and things are making so much sense. I'll pull an all-nighter and finish this report, which I know will win me an excellent grade. You should try this next time you have an essay or a research project. It's amazing." Edith turned back to her work and resumed writing.

It was obvious that her thoughts were flowing well. There were no correction marks on her paper. Although Eva was fascinated by Edith's composure, she wondered what Edith would do when she landed a full-time job and needed to concentrate her efforts. Was she going to constantly depend on drugs to make her think properly?

As for Eva, she was not going to take up Edith's offer. She made a secret vow never to engage in hard drugs. She would rather fail a class than get grades earned from mind-altering substances. She surprised herself, realizing her disdain of it all.

It was no shock when, halfway through the school year, Edith announced she was quitting university to move to another city. On her last night at the Zone, Edith declared that Eva would always be safe. Even though she was moving to another city with her boyfriend, the gang of outlaws they were part of had chapters in several major cities, including Real Mountain. Edith added that anyone who wanted to hurt Eva or hurt anyone from the Myerbell High atrium gang would have to go through her new friends first. "My friends are like secret little angels that no one sees," she stated proudly. "But they're no angels when someone threatens one of their own."

Somehow it did not make Eva feel any safer.

The next morning, as Eva shared her concern about her lost friend, Albert seemed better looking than ever. Pulling his chair close, he looked into her eyes. She leaned closer to him, and they shared a passionate kiss. He asked if she would consider studying together that night, which was a night off work for them both. She agreed, suggesting her apartment.

Albert was faring much better than her in his classes. Eva attributed it to the fact that Albert's parents helped with the bills, and Albert only needed a part-time job. He was patient and kind and reminded her of a more mature version of Mark. Their friendship was positive, and Eva enjoyed spending time with him. Studying with him between classes had proven to be advantageous for Eva, as Albert was smart and understood the concepts better. His memory was also phenomenal. However, that night they did not study much beside each other's anatomy.

For the next several weeks, they were constantly together. Albert spent more time at Eva's apartment than at his own. They ate together, slept together, studied together, and attended class together. Eva loved the attention he gave her, and it almost made her forget Lewis.

Then Christmas came. Eva realized she did not want to bring Albert home to her family. She felt uncomfortable, and the voice in her head came rushing back, telling her how much of a hypocrite she was. She tried to drown her brain in alcohol to numb the feeling of self-hatred. Just like Mark, Albert was a good guy. She just did not love him. She did not want to inflict the same pain on him that she had experienced.

When Albert shared that his parents were expecting him at their house for the holiday season, he asked if she would consider coming with him. She used the occasion to share her heart with him. With as much tact and gentleness as she could, she told him that it would be better if they no longer saw each other, as she did not see a future together. Albert was crushed. Eva knew how he felt, because the roles were reversed. She was the one saying goodbye and initiating the separation. Albert left the café, never to return.

Eva saw him again when classes resumed after the holidays, but they no longer talked or hung around. Eva was right back where she had been in September: sitting alone in the café drinking mochas while watching the infinity of cars pass by in a chorus of unpleasant noises.

8

DEAR CHARMING LEWIS

The holiday season ended, and with all the Christmas lights removed, Real Mountain's glamour started to wear off. Alone in her apartment, Eva's negative self-talk worsened. She was not doing as well as she thought she would. With Albert out of the picture, the loss of her study companion showed in her marks. She barely made the minimum passing grades, and her fear of failing was manifesting through knots in her stomach and occasional bout of nausea.

She also had trouble sleeping because of the traffic noise. Ambulance or police sirens replaced the evening crickets stridulating her to sleep, not to mention the engine brakes from big rigs, which woke her up at all hours. Eva longed for the sounds of the wind blowing through the leaves and birds chirping at sunrise in the fields, like she had experienced back home. Her idealistic views of the city were slowly crushed under the wheels of time.

Eva also developed a health condition that caused her such pain that, on occasion, she wound up in the emergency department at Real Mountain Hospital, where she would be intubated and medicated for several days. To Eva's frustration, the doctors could not diagnose any specific ailment. She decided to stop the weed and limit her alcohol intake, hoping it would help. Not having mentioned her habits to any doctor, she tried to control her drinking on her own.

She felt more attracted to Lewis, with each Friday and Saturday nights at the Zone hanging around him. His charm caused such an emotional pull that it consumed her.

Eva noticed that he had not been serious with any girls since his arrival at Real Mountain. She interpreted it as a desire to engage in a serious relationship with her, especially considering the recent developments between them.

April was coming fast, and so were final exams, which counted for 75% of her overall grade.

One night, on the pretext of needing to get away from all the stress of studying, Lewis invited Eva to sit with him in a small booth at the Zone. For the first time, he made clear advances to her. One drink led to another and Lewis invited Eva to visit his fraternity house. Already a little tipsy, she agreed with delight. The adventure of visiting a male dorm where girls were not allowed evoked a thrill that she had not felt in a long time.

Eva giggled and laughed louder than she ought. Lewis hushed her as he also laughed, holding her hand as they tiptoed to the side of the building, where a window was ajar. Lewis opened it wider and motioned for Eva to jump in first. She plunged in headfirst, only to be stuck halfway, her bum sticking out. Laughing even more, Lewis pushed on her bum, causing Eva to lose a sandal as she dropped onto the floor of the dark room. It was an empty office that was used for storage. The lights were off, but it was easy to see the shadow of boxes and old furniture from the streetlight coming through the windows void of any curtains or blinds. Lewis got in, sandal in hand.

Lewis replaced her shoe, silently mimicking the prince in the Cinderella story, and then led the way across the dark room toward the exit.

Once in the hall, they looked around to see if anyone had been alerted by the commotion. Reassured, they headed for the stairs, which led to Lewis's floor.

Lewis turned on the lights in the stairway and hallways, displayed his usual self-assurance, no longer afraid of being caught. No one from his floor would say anything, since all the boys would gladly welcome a female to their room. However, that night, no one was in the hall, and every door was closed.

Placing his index on her mouth, Lewis signalled her not to talk and to walk quietly. He did not want all the boys to come out of their rooms to see who was with him.

As they walked across the hall to Lewis's room, they heard noises of all kinds echoing in the hallway. A stereo system was playing hard rock music while a ball thumped against a wall. She also heard laughter and loud talking. Smells of all kinds emanated from the rooms. Some was good cooking, others were old, dirty socks. Her senses were tickled. Eva felt ecstatic.

Reaching the other end of the hall, Lewis opened the door to his room. He pulled Eva inside and shut the door behind her. They both broke out in a sigh of relief and laughter.

The small room was furnished with two narrow beds, one against each wall. The beds were adorned with what Eva considered ugly bed covers, which matched the curtains over the room's single window. Beneath it were two small bedside tables. The window faced the door, which was flanked by two small desks. The small wardrobe door was ajar, revealing somewhat of a mess.

Sensing she was not impressed with his living quarters, Lewis embraced her passionately to recapture her attention. She forgot her surroundings and abandoned herself in his virile arms, savouring each breath of intimacy. At long last, she welcomed every touch of his embracing hands.

They had fallen asleep and were awoken by Lewis's roommate entering. "Is it that late?" Lewis mumbled, half asleep and annoyed by the interruption. His roommate rolled his eyes, knowing Lewis was not ignorant of the time. His roommate threw himself in his own bed and started snoring within minutes. Eva felt uncomfortable with the threesome. Realizing how small Lewis's bed was, she whispered that it might be better if she went home. Lewis agreed. They got dressed and then walked back down the stairs.

As they walked back to her apartment, the city slowly began to awaken, and they saw the first signs of daylight in the sky.

"We should do this again," Lewis said, smiling. "It was fun."

Eva stopped and stared at him. Was that what he thought of her, someone to have fun with? "What do you mean?" she replied stoically.

"You know, what we did tonight. It was fun, and it's good to have fun once in a while. Don't you want to enjoy some fun?"

Eva was too hurt to respond. She had been a fool. She should have known Lewis was a one-night-stand kind of guy. He had never been with a girl for long periods of time. He consumed girlfriends like children consume candies. She was just another conquest. It was as if the fog in her brain vanished instantly. She did not feel tipsy anymore, and the pain of the hole in her heart was so intense that she could hardly breathe. She slapped him in the face and then ran up to her apartment where she cried herself to sleep.

Natasha was worried. She had not heard from Eva all day, and she was MIA from the traditional Friday night dart contest at the Zone. She decided to head to Eva's apartment, since Eva had not called back in response to several messages Natasha had left her. Lewis's evasive response to her probing confirmed her suspicions.

When she unlocked Eva's door with her spare key, she found her in her bed sleeping in an abnormal tranquility. Natasha started to panic when she realized Eva had over-sedated herself with sleeping pills. She tried to count what was left in the open container and realized with horror that a deadly quantity was missing. She called 911 and tried to wake Eva by shaking her. Eva moved slowly, talking incoherently in a weak voice. By that time, Natasha was following the 911 dispatcher's instructions in an attempt to save Eva's life as the ambulance rushed to her apartment.

Once at the hospital, after her stomach was pumped and her condition stabilized, Eva lay in bed, resting. Alone and staring at the walls, which were as white as those in her apartment, she thought of her life. In mutiny, her heart told her how much of a failure she was. She was not beautiful, desirable, or important. Mark no longer wanted her. Lewis never cared for her. She hated her job and hated living in Real Mountain even more. Her apartment was ugly, and she didn't have much money. University bills were piling up, and there was no assurance she was even going to pass her first year. She had gotten herself in so much debt that she was suffocating. Everything in her life was wrong. She was ashamed of what she had done. She hated herself for having failed her third suicide attempt and hated herself even more for the fact that she knew she lacked the courage to try again. She did not know what to do. She wanted to get away. She could not stand living like that anymore.

The doctor entered the room, interrupting her thoughts. He asked her how she felt. She lied through her teeth, saying she was fine. With all the psychology theories she had memorized over the past eight months, she knew exactly what to say and how to manipulate the doctor into signing her release papers. She was sent home within the hour.

The semester ended with Eva barely making the grades. Natasha had proven to be a good friend. However, Eva avoided the Zone at all costs, preferring to drink alone rather than risk seeing Lewis. She did not feel like hanging out with the gang anymore. She was hurting too much.

Having moved from the kitchen to the living room, Eva sat comfortably on her old couch. Putting down the last of her journals, she drank the last sip of coffee. She knew that the night before had not been an exception to what she had just read. Alone in her apartment she drank so much that she'd passed out in the early hours of the morning. *So much for trying to moderate my drinking habits,* she thought. She remembered that the day before, someone had come to her door and then left. She wondered who it could have been. Natasha maybe? No, she would have used her spare key. She did not know and did not even care anymore.

Through the living room window, the early morning sun was rising. Classes were over for the summer, and most of her friends were busy working full-time jobs. Eva picked up a pen and wrote a new entry in her journal. "April 28. What am I doing here? I hate my job, I hate this place, and I hate the Zone, because everyone is a friend of Lewis, and no one cares that he is an idiotic, arrogant donkey. And no one cares that he hurt me so bad." She closed with her traditional signature: "The Black Sheep."

It was too early to call Natasha, so she headed back to the kitchen to make a fresh pot of coffee. While it brewed, she placed two slices of bread in the toaster. The doorbell rang again.

This time, Eva opened the door promptly. "What are you doing up so early?" Eva exclaimed as she greeted her best friend. Natasha was worried for her, as she had not heard from Eva for a few days. Natasha had been working double shifts and had been unable to come for a visit.

"And since you don't have an answering machine," Natasha said, "I couldn't reach you. You never answer your phone!" Eva replied that she had unplugged her phone a few days before and forgot to plug it back in. Brushing off her explanation, Natasha carried on. "I need to talk with you. I have something important to share with you."

As she sat down at the kitchen table, Natasha handed Eva a small white bag that contained a book. "This was in the hall in front of your door. Somebody must have left it there."

Eva tossed it on the kitchen counter without even looking at it. She was much more interested in what her best friend had to say.

"I know what happened the night of the party," Natasha said, her face serious and her tone solemn.

Eva looked perplexed. "What do you mean?"

"You know . . . the wine party you don't remember anything about besides getting there with Mark and waking up at his place the next morning. The party with Edith and Lewis?"

Eva's eyes grew bigger. "What do you mean 'Lewis'? Lewis was there?" Eva leaned forward, giving Natasha her full attention.

Natasha had managed to extort the truth out of Lewis a few days after Eva's recent trip to the hospital, so she began to unfold Lewis's confession.

When Mark and Eva arrived at the party, about thirty-five people were already there, including Lewis and Bobby. Wine was flowing, as the theme of the evening was red wine. Eva remembered that part, because a song about red wine had been playing when they arrived, and it had caught her attention.

A few glasses of wine later, Mark went to the kitchen to get more. Since he was lingering, Lewis saw an opportunity to help his friend hit a homerun with his girlfriend by spiking her glass with something to arouse her. Lewis got what he needed from Bobby and dropped it into a full glass of red wine.

Lewis sat beside Eva and handed her the spiked glass while engaging in conversation. He noticed her gaze changing and her eyes becoming red. Without warning, Eva blurted out to Lewis how she had loved him all these years and wanted him to be her boyfriend. As she leaned forward to kiss him, Mark arrived. Lewis got up quickly and told Mark that Eva was drunk. Lewis pretended to be clueless as to the cause of her behaviour and left the room as he witnessed Eva throwing herself into Mark's arms while trying to kiss her boyfriend and repeating the same words that she had just uttered seconds before to Lewis: "I love you. I always loved you."

Confused and in shock at what he had just witnessed, Mark tried to talk to Eva to clarify what had just happened. He grabbed her arm impatiently and pulled her aside. But Eva was incoherent and looked like she was about to pass out. Mark brought her to his place, considering she was in no condition to go home. Eva knew the rest. She entered Mark's apartment and went straight to the bathroom to vomit and then passed out.

Eva was stupefied. She understood how it must have been hurtful for Mark to see his girlfriend throw herself into the arms of his best friend and then try unskilfully to make him believe her loving words were meant for him. Eva was embarrassed at the way Mark found out that she had never truly loved him but was—unbeknownst even to her—enamoured with a disgusting jerk. Eva felt pain for Mark. She was also enraged that Lewis had drugged her. The idea that someone had laced her drink made her feel dirty and violated.

She was no longer hungry. Now she felt sick. She pushed her peanut-butter-and-jelly sandwich aside and looked at Natasha. "What do I do now?"

"I don't know," Natasha replied. Eva thought that speaking with Mark would make things worse, because it was true that she had been in love with Lewis all along. Knowing Lewis's true nature now, she recognized how foolish she had been. Mark was a good guy. Lewis was a macho womanizer. She hated Lewis for who he was and for what he had done to her and to Mark.

Eva redirected her attention to her best friend. "Someone came to my door yesterday morning and buzzed several times. Was it you?" Natasha shook her head and suggested it could have been anyone from the gang who noticed her absence. Everyone had been worried about her.

As she headed to the door, Natasha told Eva she would ask around and let her know if anyone they knew had come.

After Natasha left, Eva returned to bed, alternating between fits of anger and outbursts of tears. She hated herself and Lewis. The negative self-talk started again, louder and harsher: *You're an idiot, Eva. You sure screwed things up. You would be better off dead.* But Eva was not going to veer onto that self-destructive path again, not this time.

She needed a distraction, something exciting that would take her mind off work, school, and particularly guys. As she lay in bed, she started contemplating skydiving. She reasoned it was the ultimate sport and that it would be a fun new experience.

Impulsively, she fetched the telephone book and looked in the section on skydiving. She found a number, dialled it, and a man answered. He said he would arrange for someone to pick her up the following Saturday morning and take her to the small local airport.

Thoughtlessly, Eva had invited a perfect stranger to pick her up from the city and bring her to a nearby town she had never heard of. All she was thinking about was skydiving. Before the telephone call, she felt emotionally drained. With this new hope of adventure, she regained excitement.

On Saturday morning at the agreed-upon time, she waited outside at the café. An old, rusty pickup truck smelling of gas a mile away came down the street. After exchanging their names,

Eva entered the truck. It was full of filthy magazines, old papers, and garbage. It smelled of gasoline, and the vinyl covering the seats was torn in various places. Eva chose to ignore the state of the truck and engaged in polite conversation with her host. Although he did not jump himself, he was part owner of the small airport and was friends with the two instructors.

The airport consisted of a small building, twenty by thirty feet, that housed a mini kitchen, a bathroom, and a big sitting area. Only Cessna planes flew in and out, as the landing strip was too short for bigger planes.

The day went by fast as Eva learned all the proper steps to jumping out of a plane and, more particularly, landing without getting hurt.

Then came the moment she had been waiting for. As she entered the Cessna, she was so excited she could hardly contain herself. The plane lifted into the air with everyone in it smiling.

Once the pilot signalled to the instructor that they had arrived at the right altitude, the instructor tapped Eva on her shoulder, indicating it was time to jump. She placed her feet in the right place and held onto the wing strut with both hands. At her instructor's command, she let go and, bam! There she was, in the air, chute wide open.

Eva admired the vastness of the globe, looking as far as her eyes could see. The high the experience provided gave her such a thrill that it made her forget everything else. She landed without a scratch and kissed the ground. "This is what I've been looking for all my life!" she yelled.

Eva spent the rest of her summer weekends at the airport. Her skydiving acquaintances helped her improve her skills.

When university resumed in the fall, Eva reluctantly ended her favourite sport to attend to her studies. However, her motivation for academics had dropped dramatically. The fall semester felt uninspiring, each class dull and unexciting. One psychology class after another, mandatory courses, optional courses, it was a long list of never-ending essays and exams. That was, until she met Jason.

9

ESCAPE TO EUROPE

J ason was a vibrant, energetic guy Eva met in one of her classes. He was a few inches shorter than her, but his laughter and sense of humour made Eva forget his diminutive size. Jason made great efforts to be with Eva and quickly shared his feelings for her. In early December, he asked her to be his girlfriend, insisting on the seriousness of the request by adding that he wanted a long-term relationship. Eva replied that she was not ready for that kind of commitment and asked for more time. They had occasional intimate times together, during which Eva hesitantly reconsidered his request.

After a romantic supper at Jason's apartment on Valentine's Day, Eva cautiously expressed her desire to become more serious with him. To her bewilderment, he responded by alluding to his friendship with a mutual female friend and how their friendship was transforming into something that caused him to be confused about his relationship with Eva. Feeling betrayed, Eva asked if he was still interested in bringing their relationship to another level. He said no, because he was confused about her and the other girl. Crushed, she returned to her apartment in tears, realizing that while he had been with her, he had also been with another girl.

Eva was angry with herself and felt bitter toward Jason. She called the other girl in an attempt to obtain closure. It was past midnight, but Eva didn't care. "You won," she said. "You get the spoils. Jason is yours."

The other girl told Eva that she had it all wrong. Her relationship with Jason was not what Eva thought, and she was not sure if she would consider being serious with him. The conversation caused more confusion than closure.

The next day, Eva put a stop to the relationship with Jason, asking him never to communicate with her again. Then she drowned herself in her studies and alcohol. She finished second year by the skin of her teeth. When mid-April came, she was at the end of her rope.

She reflected on all that she had gone through in the past few years and tried to make sense of her life. She had looked to ease the pain of her relationship with her father with alcohol and weed, but both had made things worse. She had tried to fill the hole in her heart with boyfriends, yoga, a therapist, fortune telling, skydiving, and busyness, but nothing had worked. She had even tried to kill herself three times, without success. She was out of ideas. She wished for another life—any life, just not hers.

Then she experienced an epiphany. That was it! She was going to live another life by going away to another country— far, far away. She called the newspaper and placed an advertisement to sell her car. It proved successful. Within three days, her car sold. She gave notice on her apartment, sold her furniture, and placed the rest of her meagre belongings in storage. Everything she needed for her trip fit into an army-size backpack. She quit her job with great joy and purchased an open-ended round-trip ticket to Europe.

A week later, she was at the Real Mountain International Airport, determined to find her new self. She concluded that she had lost her identity while searching for a boyfriend or being in a relationship. She was going to be alone and stay alone in order to enjoy life.

Natasha and George accompanied her to the airport. Natasha confirmed that no one from the gang had come to her house the day Eva had heard the buzzer. Eva no longer wished to solve the mystery. She was heading to Europe for a new life. She was not even sure when she would return or if she would return at all.

As she said her goodbyes, she told George to take care of Natasha and then headed off to the security checkpoint. After a last wave on the other side, she walked to her gate, an announcement for her flight already underway.

Eva decided to visit as many countries as possible. After taking a train to the centre of Paris, the city of love, she opened her map, closed her eyes, and dropped her finger. When she opened her eyes, she saw where her finger had landed. *Bruges! I'll hitchhike to Belgium,* she thought. *Wow! That'll be an adventure.*

Away from it all and with no possibility of being contacted except by general mail delivery, Eva felt free. Since no one knew which country she was in, who could send her letters anyway? She loved the freedom and the absence of her father's comments about danger. She did not want to hear anything about danger.

Eva had purchased a Youth Hostel Association membership card. That meant she was allowed to lodge at any youth hostel in Europe at a discount price. From Bruges, she headed to Venice, where she met a sweet, handsome guy who gave her all the attention she craved. She abandoned herself in his arms. The secrecy of intimacy in a dorm room of a youth hostel where twenty other people slept was adventurous enough for Eva. She did not belong to anyone and thought it would be fun. If Lewis could do it, why not her? Besides, the guy had no expectations of a long-term relationship. They enjoyed their time together for a short period, and then Eva left for Brindisi.

She took a night train to the south of Italy. She thought she could sleep on the train and save the cost of a stay at a hostel. She arrived at the station early and was one of the first to board. Finding an empty cabin, she placed her backpack on the baggage rack and made herself as comfortable as possible for the next eight hours, thinking she would sleep most of the way.

Since it was already close to midnight, it did not take her long to doze off. She noticed a young man enter the cabin after her, but she was too tired to acknowledge him. She also heard some commotion, with someone else wanting to enter the cabin but did not clue in that her cabin buddy had prevented anyone from entering by locking the door and shutting the blinds. Eva did not see that the train was quickly filling up, but their cabin was not. She was tired and did not want to be bothered.

Not long after the train left the station, the guy's intentions were revealed. He sat next to her and started to touch her without permission. Eva jolted out of her seat, unlocked the door, and jumped out of the cabin into the crowded hallway. She asked if anyone spoke English. Getting no response, she opened the door to the next cabin. There, she saw a family of four. The father, double the size of her assailant, was a tall, muscular American soldier who looked to be in his early thirties. His wife, a pretty blonde lady, was sitting in front of him, and each had a teen boy sitting beside them.

The four of them looked at Eva, wondering what was going on. After Eva explained her situation, the man offered his seat and volunteered to retrieve her backpack, adding that he would go into her cabin to enjoy more space for a better sleep, confident that Eva's former cabin buddy was no threat to him. Eva took his seat with a thankful smile. As the soldier left, his wife assured Eva that her husband had several years of combat experience.

Moments later, Eva and the lady heard a commotion in Eva's former cabin. The assurance and calm the wife displayed reassured Eva. A few minutes later, the soldier entered the cabin with Eva's backpack. He smiled triumphantly and then went back to the other cabin to get some sleep.

In the morning, when Eva's stop was announced, she thanked her saviours profusely and then prepared to disembark. Her assailant was also outside the cabin. When he saw Eva, he tried to attack her again, this time more furiously out of revenge for his previous defeats with her and with the American soldier. However, the train was still full of people, and several other men, including the soldier, prevented him from touching her. In anger, Eva yelled the only word she knew in Italian, "Vafanc***!" Without waiting for his response and without noticing the looks of disapproval on the faces of the men who rescued her, she ran out the door as the train came to a halt.

Foul language had come out of her mouth increasingly since she moved to Real Mountain. Away from her parents, she considered herself free to unleash her anger. Swearing made her feel tough and gave her a sense of strength that masked her fears and insecurities. She knew she had said an insulting and vulgar word that all the Italian people on the train disapproved of. However, Eva didn't care. She had been attacked physically, and she had retaliated the only way she could: with words.

Still agitated and furious about the ordeal, she walked toward the youth hostel. She would have plenty of time to cool down, as the hostel was located two hours from the train station. It was nestled in the hills, away from the town and beach.

Eva had never tasted a better café latte, and her stay was a welcomed reprieve. But the monotony of the peaceful Italian country life prompted Eva to move on. Only a few days after her arrival, she hit the road again.

Eva decided to take the Brindisi/Patras ferry across the Mediterranean to reach Athens. Once again, she decided to take the night ferry to save another night at the hostel. The sixteen-hour trip would be easy and cheap, as she did not take a cabin. She planned to linger around the bridge for the duration of the trip. That way, no one would bother her.

While on the ferry, Eva met a guy her age who was traveling with his two sisters and their long-time friend. They invited Eva to join them. They were also heading toward Athens and planned on going to Mykonos Island afterward. Eva agreed wholeheartedly, laughingly nicknaming the five of them the "Fantastic Five." They were nice to her but often argued amongst themselves. Eva wasn't used to siblings' spats and didn't enjoy the squabbling. But it never lasted long and was never serious.

Athens was noisier than Real Mountain, and as much as Eva enjoyed being in a foreign city, she looked forward to Mykonos Island.

The ferry trip took eight hours. As soon as they stepped off, a man approached them, talking loudly in broken English. He appeared agitated. The five of them looked at each other, unsure how to respond. Puzzled by his behaviour, and thinking the man would not understand her, Eva asked her new acquaintances if they understood why he was angry with them. The man understood what she'd said, and instantly changed his expression and smiled. "I'm not angry," he said in clearer English. "This is how we talk here. You must come to my hotel and stay. It is located on the other side of the island, where it is quiet and pleasant, and I will give you a good price." They all looked at each other and agreed. A good price was a language the Fantastic Five could understand.

The innkeeper had not lied. His hotel was clean, quiet, and pleasant. The five slept in the same room—the two sisters in one bed, the two boys in another, and Eva on an improvised cot.

The next day at breakfast, the innkeeper informed them that sharks had been sighted, rendering swimming dangerous on that side of the island. The Fantastic Five decided to head toward the beach nonetheless, since the famous Mykonos beaches were located on the other side of the island.

They had three beaches to choose from. The sisters and the two boys decided to stay at the first beach. Eva took a small boat to the second beach, planning to swim back to the first beach, where the others would wait for her. She left wearing only her monokini.

Ignoring the warnings, she headed toward the sea as soon as the boat landed on the second beach. She swam along the peninsula that separated the beaches. After several hours of swimming, she reached the first beach and joined the rest of the group.

Eva mocked her father in her mind, knowing he would have prevented her from doing what she had just done. She was exulting with joy that he was not there to deprive her of adventure and fun. She had just proven that there was no danger.

That afternoon, she met a guy at the beach who was from Athens. He displayed interest in her and was courteous. He showed her the town and spent a great deal of time answering her questions about history and culture. Eva felt safe enough with him to share her fantasy of spending a night of intimacy on a beach. He said he would make her dream come true. And he did.

In the early morning, just before sunrise, Eva returned to the hostel alone and disappointed. It had been the second time she had dreamed of something romantic, intimate, and lovely only to have it turn into a disaster. There had been nothing great about doing it on the beach. It had actually been uncomfortable and unpleasant. Movies were a lie, and Eva had been a fool to believe them.

The few weeks of holidays were over for the rest of the group. They needed to return to Athens. From there, they made their way back to Italy, where they said their goodbyes. Eva was tired of the sisters and brother always arguing anyway. She wanted some quiet time to herself.

On the train, she met a girl heading home to Lucerne, Switzerland. She invited Eva to her apartment. Eva agreed, with gratitude.

While in Lucerne, Eva took several train rides back and forth across the country to explore some of the little towns, like Gruyères, where she ate the famous cheese with wine, and Lausanne, where she visited a museum. Becoming bored once more, she thanked her new friend and moved on to Germany.

After a short stay, she headed back south. Fall was approaching, and she did not want to feel the cold. The fall reminded her of home and what she was desperately trying to forget. So she fled the north and headed toward the south of France.

She found the beach in Saint-Tropez disappointing. The TV shows and movies seriously overrated the place, she thought, and felt once again, naïve for having believed what she had seen in movies. That was before she had a long conversation with the owner of a local bistro on the beachfront. He explained that the beach was much more interesting during the high tourist season. Had Eva arrived earlier in the spring, she would have had an entirely different experience. But the tourist season was over now and the beach was deserted. "In the spring," the gentleman added, "you could have been hired as a waitress and would have made good money." Eva pondered the idea for a moment and wished she could go back in time.

She stayed in Saint-Tropez for a short while, just long enough to meet four Norwegian guys who displayed gentlemanly interest in her. They were muscular and well built, and Eva found them all attractive, particularly with their blue eyes and blond hair. The four of them could have made the cover of a fashion magazine. After a long conversation about their country of origin and life aspirations, they decided to go swimming. Taking off her shirt and Bermuda shorts to reveal her monokini, Eva ran into the sea.

The four gentlemen stood there in shock before quickly regaining their composure and joining her in the ocean, laughing and playing. Later that day, understanding that Eva was travelling alone, they took it upon themselves to protect her. They explained that traveling alone was dangerous, and that they feared for her safety. They offered to shelter her for the night in one of their tents (while they occupied the other). Eva was touched by the sacrifice they made for her. The four guys would be packed like sardines in one tent, while she would be comfortable in the other. She took up their offer, thinking she was saving the price of a night at a youth hostel. After thanking them profusely the next day, she left for Barcelona. Eva did not feel like hanging around four replicas of her father.

In Barcelona, Eva met Francis. He was also a tourist travelling in Europe. He explained that he was from a small town in the middle of nowhere that no one knew about. Eva replied that she was also from a small town he had probably never heard of. When Francis stated he was from Myerbell, Eva's jaw dropped. Francis had also attended Myerbell High, though a decade before her.

He had a spinal malformation that caused him to be a bit hunchbacked. Eva did not mind though, because his blue eyes and blond hair compensated nicely. She considered him attractive. Having just handed in his master's thesis, he was spending some vacation time before heading back to Real Mountain, where a good job was waiting for him. His trip was coming to a close, his return flight departing in three days. Eva felt an instant attraction to him.

They spent the rest of his time in Spain together. Eva was mesmerized by his assurance and maturity. When

Francis left for the airport, she promised to connect as soon as she returned. They shared a passionate kiss just before his taxi took him away.

Eva decided to head back to Paris. When she arrived, she was out of money. Her three days with Francis had incurred unexpected expenses. They had stayed at a nice hotel, which was much costlier than a youth hostel. Francis's restaurant choices were also much more luxurious than Eva's "bread and cheese on the fly" meals. And since Francis was a modern guy, they shared the cost of everything equally. She reluctantly decided to call her parents.

Her mom picked up the phone, obviously pleased to hear from her daughter. However, Eva sensed she was also striving to conceal her worries about Eva's whereabouts.

After a few pleasantries, because Eva did not want her parents to know about all the things she had done or people she had met, she asked if she could borrow some money. Her mother agreed without hesitation. Her father also asked how his little girl was doing. He insisted that the amount she requested was not enough and that he preferred sending double to ensure her safety. He mentioned that he and her mother were praying for her to have a safe trip. Eva confirmed to which post office they should send their money order and thanked them gratefully.

After hanging up Eva was amazed yet again by her father's attitude. She no longer recognized him. He was so attentive and nice. She did not know what to think.

IO

REAL MOUNTAIN REALITY

After getting the extra money, Eva felt the freedom to stay longer in Europe. However, she also felt the void of Francis's absence. She had been on the road for most of the summer and had a few adventures under her belt, but none compared with the time she'd spent with Francis. He was so sure of himself. She was excited that such a handsome and grown-up man would want her.

The week after his departure, as she wandered around Paris, she met a photographer, who was also a journalist. He sold articles about his various trips. It was lucrative enough to pay for everything he needed and enabled him to travel across the world. After some time together, he invited Eva to go to the Eiffel Tower.

They talked at length. He expressed in no uncertain terms his interest in her. He told Eva that she was attractive and that he would like to offer her the opportunity to work as his assistant/model, explaining she could be in his photographs and in his next articles. All Eva had to do was agree to stay with him on his various trips around the world, and he would pay for everything.

Flattered, Eva was tempted. After he explained that he wanted them to live as a couple, she asked if she could get back to him the following day. Her plan was to call Francis, ask him how serious he was about her, and then decide whether to stay with the photographer or return home to be with Francis.

Francis's response was clear. He missed her and wanted her in his life. She asked if he would consider moving in together. He agreed enthusiastically. However, because of the bad quality of the telephone lines and the cost of lengthy conversation, they did not discuss the details of their arrangements, and Eva did not mention the exact date she would return. She turned down the journalist's offer, explaining that she was returning home.

Within a week, she was back at Real Mountain International Airport. Since she had been unable to reach Francis on the telephone, she reluctantly called her parents. Her father offered to pick her up. She saw him as she came down the escalator toward baggage claim, smiling, his arms wide open. He hugged her so hard she almost choked. He was glad she had returned home safely. After picking up her backpack, they drove home. Eva had nowhere to go. With no car, apartment, job, or money, she was at the mercy of her parents, and she did not like it at all.

As soon as they arrived home, Eva tried reaching Francis once again. This time, he picked up. After confirming she was back in the country, she asked if she could move with him right away. He responded favourably, but she sensed a bit of a surprise in his voice. She brushed off any sense that he was not as thrilled as her, and asked her father, who had just brought in her backpack in, if he could return it to the car. She was heading straight back to Real Mountain and at a new address. Obviously disappointed, he brought her to Francis's apartment.

After a few days together, Eva fully disclosed her dire financial situation. Francis was surprised and openly displayed his displeasure. He asked how she was going to pay her share of the rent and, with disapproval in his tone, expressed that, in Europe, she had led him to believe she was financially comfortable. He added that their Europe arrangement of sharing the financial load fifty-fifty remained. Eva felt like an elementary school child being scolded by her teacher.

Francis told her to find a job quickly, then rolled his eyes in contempt and walked away from the kitchen. Then he sighed while heading toward the living room to sit in front of the television. As he did, he mumbled something about how she had better not expect him to pay for her. Eva was dumbfounded.

Jobless and having sold everything of value before leaving for Europe, coupled with the fact that she was already severely in debt from her tuition fees and now owed money to her parents, she reluctantly admitted that returning to university was out of the question. Closing that door pinched her heart.

But she was convinced she could find a job quickly, and so headed toward the employment office in search of a decent job. With only two years of post-secondary education, Eva could not afford to be picky. But she was bilingual and living in a city where most government positions required bilingualism. She was hired within a week.

That same week, she also found a part-time evening job as a waitress in a fancy downtown restaurant. She was quite proud of herself.

Francis raised his eyebrow. He was not impressed. It was as if her finding two jobs within a week was nothing. Eva got the impression that she was not enough in herself, that whatever she thought or said or did was never going to be enough for him.

To save money, Eva cancelled her storage contract and picked up all her belongings, bringing them to Francis's apartment by taxi. They included six large cardboard boxes. Without unpacking them, she went down to the basement to put them in the large cabinet assigned to their apartment number, right next to the washer and dryer. Eva did not care about the basement humidity. Somehow, in the depth of her heart, she already knew she was not going to be with Francis for long, but she refused to acknowledge it.

She also refused to acknowledge something else, something important. She had repressed in her subconscious that she had always wanted to become a psychologist, and quitting school only proved she was one of those weak ones that her Psychology 101 teacher had talked about. She was now part of the losers' group.

The negative self-talk felt like a vulture breathing down her neck. *You're a failure. You need to try harder, be better and do more.* In an attempt to shut up the negative self-talk, she started to rationalize how her newfound employment was going to change her relationship. Trying to convince herself that she was in love, she concluded that she needed to invest in the relationship to make it work. And making good money at both jobs would raise Francis's view of her.

Being in the office all day and at the restaurant most evenings left little time for the alleged investment in their relationship. In addition, Eva worked every second weekend. She had lost touch with Natasha from having been gone for so long. Now she felt a big chasm separating them. She suspected Natasha felt it too. Natasha was still with George, and the last time Eva heard from them, they were talking about marriage. They were still pursuing their full-time studies and working at the same time, making Natasha incredibly busy. Eva wanted to spend as much time as her schedule allowed investing in her relationship with Francis; she had no time to spare for any other relationships. This made her feel vulnerable and alone, but she wasn't prepared to admit it.

Additionally, Eva had started distancing herself from the gang before she left for Europe. Francis's apartment was at the other end of the city, which made it complicated and time-consuming to reach the Zone by bus. Francis adamantly refused to go to the Zone, considering it an immature waste of time. He also refused to lend his car to Eva, alluding again to her immaturity. Eva felt hurt and humiliated. Sometimes he mocked her emotions and compared her to a teenager. Eva didn't dare talk about returning to skydiving, for fear he would criticize her taste in sports.

As fall went by, Eva felt increasingly lonely in the relationship, and at the same time, Francis turned distant. It became obvious that while Eva was working at the restaurant, he would go out. Eva did not know with whom or where. She felt left out and wondered why, when they had time together, Francis refused to go out with her, but when she was not around, he enjoyed going out with other people. He never introduced her to anyone he knew, as if he was embarrassed about her.

The Sunday before Christmas holidays, Eva was waiting at home for Francis to return from yet another of his mysterious escapades. He had left in the early hours of the morning while she was still sleeping, and it was now 6:00 p.m. He had not called or left a note.

When he entered the apartment, she made a huge scene, screaming at him for not letting her know where he was. She accused him of not investing in their relationship. He was hiding who he was with and what he had done. She demanded that he tell the truth. He said he had spent the day skating with a female colleague.

"There's no way you skated from eight in the morning to six at night," she said. "What else have you done with her?"

He looked at her mockingly and brushed her off, stating she was acting like a teenager again. He went into the living room, turned on the TV, and sat on the couch, ignoring her.

That's when it hit her. Eva relived in her head the many altercations she had had with her father, particularly when she was a teenager. Francis was just like her father. She could not believe she had fallen for such a guy.

They spent the holiday season separately. Then, on the first Saturday of January, she moved out of his place into a small studio/bachelor apartment closer to work. The apartment came fully furnished, including dishes in the cupboards and old pots and pans in the oven drawer. Since she had all that she needed, she piled her six cardboard boxes in the storage space of her new apartment building.

On her first night, she fell asleep, sobbing in disappointment, frustration, and anger. By that time, her government job was taking too much of her energy. She no longer felt the need to impress anyone with her resourcefulness, so she quit the waitressing job to focus on her government career.

Within a week, she realized her life was a complete train wreck. She decided to attend meetings for those who had parents who were dysfunctional. Ironically, the group reminded her of the one she had attended a few years back when her father had given his "testimony."

Her pride somewhat crushed and her tail between her legs, Eva went every week. The group promoted abstinence from drugs and alcohol. Eva thought it was a group for her, as she had concluded that she was messed up, because her parents messed up her life. She had experienced firsthand how drugs and alcohol only provided temporary relief and brought her more trouble than good.

The group consisted of approximately thirty people who met weekly. Several members were significantly older than her, and the few her age were in a relationship. Three ladies hung around together all the time. Being her mother's age, they took it upon themselves to make Eva feel at home. However, one gentleman intrigued her. He was handsome and respectful and often complimented her. He listened to her and liked to be with her.

Sean was fifteen years older than Eva, but she did not mind. She rationalized that fact, tried to convince herself that Sean was not at all like Francis and that age had nothing to do with compatibility.

Spring came, and the self-help group was helping Eva see why she did what she did and why she was like she was. The members were all friendly and non-judgemental. It was refreshing. Sean increasingly displayed affection toward her; however, Eva ensured their relationship stayed platonic. Sean's views on material things were different from hers, and it put a damper in her attraction toward him.

Sean believed everyone should live in communes, and that no one should own valuable personal belongings. Having done some mission work in the past, he despised the rich. Eva was not dreaming of becoming luxuriously rich, but she was not ready to make a vow of poverty either. Long gone were her dreams of becoming a nun. She definitely did not see herself living in the same house as other families and sharing everything.

Eva dreamed of country living. She wanted to own a property furnished with all the latest items, where she would live with her family. Sean also wanted to have a family and live in the country but in a commune setting like hippies of the 1960s. He loved children and longed to have many. Eva felt they had enough things in common to hang onto the relationship. She preferred to focus on what they had in common than what divided them. She vowed to go slow and wait before becoming intimate with him. Since he respected her boundaries, they got along well.

Eva's government career was thriving. Within eighteen months, she had obtained a promotion that provided a substantive increase in salary. From the outside, she looked like she was accomplished. Her career was moving ahead better than expected. She was getting along with her coworkers, and her relationship with her parents had never been so positive.

The long winter was coming to an end, and Eva was moving into a bigger and better apartment.

She moved by herself, taking a taxi back and forth to transport her six boxes and then some. The store from which she had purchased her furniture was delivering it all that same day. While she waited, she unpacked her boxes. Noticing the last box had worn-out corners and that dust had found its way in, Eva considered throwing away the content. Until she realized it contained her old diaries and a white plastic bag with something square and hard in it.

She pondered it for a moment, wondering how the white bag had made it into her personal things. Then she opened the bag out of curiosity and found a small hardcover book. That was when it all came back to her. This was the white bag that had been left outside the door of her university apartment. She had forgotten it.

Eva put the book aside to save it for later as a reward for having completed her move and continued unpacking the remainder of her things. She wanted her apartment to look nice and clean. It was newly renovated, and the new furniture she'd purchased with the bit of money she'd saved made it look clean and homey. She was proud of the decor she had managed to whip into shape with the few resources she had. She was going to be comfortable, and her new salary was sufficient.

As Eva organized everything, her mind was somewhere else. She was struggling emotionally. The only aspect of her life that was going well was her job, which was the only stability in her life. She still had university debts, which made things tight financially. Although she got along with her colleagues, they were not friends. The support group helped, but

Eva still felt empty. She had a nagging feeling of emptiness that booze or drugs could not remove, a constant feeling that she was not enough: not good enough, not smart enough, not pretty enough. It was driving her crazy. She still felt a hole in her heart and was at a loss about how to fill it.

Eva recognized that whether she was in a relationship or not, the hole was still there. Even when a boyfriend complimented her, she felt ugly and unappealing. Despite her recent promotion, she felt like a failure. Nothing she had tried fixed the problem. She started to think that her wetting the bed until her late teenage years might have had something to do with it. She wasn't sure.

As she dropped her last empty cardboard box into the garbage bin, she looked at her apartment and felt satisfied. Everything was in its place. She was home. The neighbourhood was quieter, and her apartment was on a one-way street, away from main boulevards. There was a small park nearby, and a bicycle path was at her door. It was a one-bedroom apartment, but the rooms were comfortable enough.

After a well-deserved supper, she decided to look into the little book in the white bag. Sitting on her brand-new, natural, off-white 100%-cotton futon, she opened the book. It was small, but several hundred pages long. The black cover had no title except the words "Volume II." Only two words were engraved in gold letters on the edge of the book: "The Author."

Eva's curiosity was piqued more than ever. Disappointed she only had the second volume, she wondered if she would understand it, not having read the first.

She opened the book and noticed there was no date or printing company address. It was as if the book had been handmade but in a professional way—it looked like any book in a store. Yet there were no indications of where it came from. Eva thought the company that printed it was bad at marketing. Anyone printing a book would want to advertise where a reader could procure more copies.

Not expecting much, Eva started reading: "You who searched in everything and anything, you who tried with every atom of your being, you who are at a loss and out of resources or ideas, to you I say meet me and your life will never be the same."

She stopped. How could this strange book know her so well? How could someone she had never met describe with such clarity and knowledge the deep longing of her heart? Who was this "Author," who was able to capture with just the dedication page what she had been looking for all her life?

11

MEETING WITH THE "ONE"

Shaking her head in disbelief, she resumed reading.

"You who searched in everything and anything, you who tried with every atom of your being, you who are at a loss and out of resources or ideas, to you I say meet me, and your life will never be the same. Meet me, and you will never fear again. Meet me, and you will never feel empty again. I can save you, heal you, and restore you. I can, and I want to. But I will respect your choice. I will not move against your will. If you allow me, I will transform your life in a way you cannot fathom. If you let me change you, the depth of your being will be unrecognizable. Let me be your guide, your strength, and your peace. Stop searching in every direction, and start seeking me. I may surprise you. I will not disappoint you. Trust me.

– The Author

"Trust me?" Eva said with skepticism. "How can I trust someone I don't know?" she added, as if someone was next to her, listening. "The nerve this Author has!" Nevertheless, she was hooked. She carried on reading while sensing a discreet tingling in her heart, like a glimpse of hope.

The first four chapters were the Author's autobiography. The rest of the chapters described how human beings are all born with an inner hole that can only be filled with the Author's love. It talked about the many humans who had misrepresented the Author with false doctrines, legalism, and religiosity. The book also talked about how much the Author wants a willing, two-sided relationship and how the Author is always willing and waiting for anyone to go to Him. The book talked about a love that is beyond any human love, a love that never fails, a love that fills and satisfies. It was all about an unconditional love that had a conditional reach; that is the willingness of the recipient to embrace it. The book also talked about how to live a life free of worry and fear.

The more Eva read the book, the more the book read her. The more she read, the more the book made sense. It included guidelines for safety and happiness. Nothing was forced or obligatory. It was simple. The book talked about the fact that the more the reader gets to know the Author, the more he or she will trust Him. The book called it "faith." The language was similar to Eva's childhood religious background, but it was so much more alive and freeing instead of being restrictive or punitive.

The Author was able to capture the essence of Eva's inner needs. The book revealed what Eva lacked and offered a long-lasting, rock-solid solution. She was mesmerized by the book and could not put it down.

Eva wanted to know more about the Author and wanted information about the first volume. Pondering who might be able to help her, she considered her parents. She wondered how they would react. She gave in, recognizing they had changed a lot in the past few years. With a bit of apprehension, Eva called her mother. To her great joy, her mother invited Eva for a visit the following weekend to discuss the book.

The workweek seemed endless. Usually enthusiastic about meeting clients and filling out government documents, Eva just wanted the week to be over. Her mind was not on her job, and it was as if each second on the clock moved slower and slower, at the pace of a dying battery.

Breaks and lunches were Eva's favourite times. Each day, she read more of her book while eating alone in a corner of the lunchroom.

When Saturday morning came, Eva hopped on a Real Mountain bus to head back to the Myerbell South bus station. She reminisced about her first trip to the city a little less than four years earlier and how she had been so excited to leave the country behind.

This time, she was looking forward to returning home, even though it was only for a few days. She was excited to talk to her parents about the book and looked forward to the peace and quiet the country provided.

As the bus entered the station, she saw her father waiting at the gate. He greeted her with a smile and his now habitual choking hug. They had not seen each other for several months, and he had missed his little girl. A little clumsy with expressions of affection, her father made an effort to ensure Eva felt comfortable and welcomed. They got in the car and drove back home for the long-awaited conversation.

Spring had come early that year, along with all its familiar sounds and smells. Eva loved the soothing noises and preferred them greatly to the groans of the city streets. The smell of the fresh air was inebriating. Eva noticed how nature exuded peace and warmed her heart. She was surprised to feel peace inside her parents' home too. For the first time in her young life, she discerned that her parents radiated peace themselves.

As they sat at the dining room table, Eva could see the bar cabinet that had been cleared of all alcohol. A bouquet of freshly cut lilacs was sitting on top of it. Each spring, her mother cut lilacs from the big bush at the west corner of the house and brought them inside for the family's olfactory enjoyment. The flowers' perfume reminded Eva of her early childhood, when things were simple and easy, when, once upon a time, her relationship with her parents was positive and pleasant—when she was daddy's little girl.

Tears formed in her eyes from the memory of all the hurts that came in her teenage years. Regaining her composure, she returned her thoughts to the purpose of her visit and got straight to the point. She pulled the book out of her purse and handed it to her mother. "I've been reading this book. Have you seen it before? Do you know what it is? Do you know who the Author is? Have you seen Volume One? If so, do you know where I can get a copy?" Eva bombarded her parents with questions, not leaving them any time to respond.

Eva's mother glanced at her husband. They exchanged a look of excitement and hope before turning back to their eager daughter. "Yes, we both have," Eva's mother replied.

Eva sighed with relief. She was finally going to get answers. In an animated tone, she asked them to explain.

It was Eva's mother who first received a copy of the same book through a friend. After reading it, her friend brought her to a gathering of friends of the Author. Gatherings, her mother explained, are places where people meet to talk about what the Author wrote in His book and how to follow in His footsteps. She suspected that someone from a gathering near her university apartment left this copy of the book at her doorstep and that the usual business card accompanying the book must have been dropped by mistake.

It took six months for Eva's father to accept his wife's persistent invitation to attend the gathering. But after giving in, he was grateful as he enjoyed attending gatherings.

Eva asked if they had addresses of other gatherings outside of Myerbell. Her mother informed her that there were gatherings everywhere in the world. She promised her daughter to get information about gatherings in Real Mountain. She explained that some gatherings were attended by only a handful of people, but others were attended by thousands, depending on where the gathering was and how open and eager people were to know the Author.

The weekend went by too fast for Eva's taste. Several years before, she had dreamed of leaving Myerbell and running away to Real Mountain; now she loathed the thought of going back to the city. But she knew she had no choice but to return to her government job.

At work, Eva was distracted. She could not wait to meet other people who had read the Author's book and wanted to talk about it.

Eva was lost in such thoughts when her telephone rang. Her mother had found the much-needed information. Gatherings of the Author's friends were held on Sunday mornings. They took place in the east end of the city in the industrial area, where few people went during the weekend. The bus service was so limited that it would take several bus transfers and a long time to get there. Eva's mother added that she knew the person in charge, and that he'd offered to have someone pick up Eva at her apartment.

Saturday night, she hardly slept. When morning came, she woke up earlier than on a normal workday, she jumped into the shower and got ready to head out.

A couple about ten years older than Eva picked her up in a clean and fairly new blue van. It was quite the contrast from her first day of skydiving. An elderly lady was also in the van. She had been picked up before Eva. The couple had three small children. The van was full.

The building was a former industrial lab transformed into an auditorium. The hallway on the left led to classrooms, each dedicated to different ages groups of children. At the end of the hallway, a kitchen and dining area served a dual purpose. Just like at NSE, the dining room was also a gym for the kids. The auditorium could hold over 300 people and was three quarters full. The seats were bright orange and looked like they came straight from the late 1960s, but they were comfortable enough.

An older gentleman came to the front stage and introduced himself as the host of the gathering. While he spoke, several young people joined him. One sat at a drum, another grabbed a guitar, a girl sat at a synthesizer, and another grabbed a microphone. Eva had not anticipated a band. In fact, she had not anticipated anything at all, since she did not know what to expect.

After the gentleman finished his introduction and welcomed everyone, the band started to play. Eva had never heard such quality music. She didn't know any of the songs, but they were lively and catchy. She found herself stamping her foot to the rhythm while clapping her hands like everybody else. Some were jumping up and down while others stayed sitting. Eva noticed how no one minded how loud or quiet the other was—everyone was focused on the front. It was like a rock show at a stadium, except no one was drunk or stoned.

After about 30 minutes of music, the band exited the stage, and the older gentleman came back to speak.

While he talked, Eva's mind wandered. Sitting in the last row at the back and knowing no one, she simply observed people. She saw that some were listening quietly while others were interacting, making comments of assent. Everyone was attentive, including the group of older teenagers sitting in the front row.

Something was floating in the air that mesmerized everyone. The children who had been singing and dancing along with the adults during the music segment had vanished in the hallway with some adults, all heading to their age-specific classes. Mothers with infants had also vanished, leaving the auditorium half empty, with people listening attentively as the older gentleman continued to speak.

Eva saw young adults her age who seemed as if their life was perfectly in order. Everyone seemed so loving, kind, and caring. It was surreal. She saw couples sitting close to each other, exuding the same kind of love she had witnessed in her parents. Eva could not believe this was real.

Then the gentleman at the front said something that brought Eva back from her drifting thoughts. He asked a question that puzzled her. "If you want to meet the Author personally, please come to the front."

Confused, Eva turned to the lady on her left. "Did I hear correctly? Did he just ask those who want to meet the Author to come to the front?"

The lady nodded, asking if Eva was interested. Eva was adamant that she wanted to meet Him. She was just surprised to discover that she could. The lady offered to accompany her to the front. A few others joined them.

The host explained that, in order to meet the Author, one needs to want to welcome him in their life. Their willingness was conditional to his response. The Author would never impose Himself on anyone. Having walked forward to the front of the gathering hall was a statement of willingness. The host asked them to repeat after him that, from now on, they would publicly declare their willingness to embrace the Author and that in response the Author would change their life for the better. From now on, they were willingly allowing the Author to lead them and strengthen them and as a result, the Author would lead them down a peaceful, fulfilling path.

After the declaration was done, more music was played while those who had come to the front were brought into another room, where a group of people awaited them. A couple greeted Eva and sat down with her on a comfortable couch. They gave Eva a book containing both volumes as they told her she was now part of the family of the Author's friends. They explained that through reading the books, Eva would get to know the Author intimately. As she got to know Him, she would trust Him more and more. They also explained that both books were written to equip the Author's friends to walk through life the way the Author had prescribed.

Eva sobbed, this time from joy. Something wonderful had happened in her heart that she could not explain. The couple reassured her that it was the effect the Author had on those who welcomed Him into their life. They experience a lifting of pain, a newfound freedom of the heart.

The more Eva and the couple talked about the Author, the more Eva felt cleansed. They explained that the Author is God and that He has various names that were described in detail in the two volumes. They further clarified that He is the Lord, the Creator of all things. He is the perfect father who knows all things. He is all-powerful. He sees everything, as He is everywhere. He is the provider for our every need. He provides peace, as He is peace. He is the protector and the deliverer in times of need. He provides healing. He is Jesus Christ The Saviour. Eva was captivated. More than ever, her interest in the Author grew strong. She did not want to go home. She wanted to hear more.

As if the couple understood what she was thinking, they reiterated the importance of reading the Author's books as often as she could, even if it was just one phrase per day. Meditating on that phrase throughout her day would help her walk in the Author's ways. Walking in the ways of His book was walking with Him. Applying what was taught in the book was to be in His presence. The couple explained that it was easier to read Volume II before Volume I. Eva's puzzled expression cued the couple to elaborate.

With patience and kindness, they explained that to better understand and appreciate Volume I it was helpful to first read Volume II, as Volume II is an accomplishment of what Volume I was foretelling. Volume I is filled with mysteries and stories that are a foreshadow of those of Volume II. Although Eva was not sure she agreed with the logic, the serenity in their tone reassured her. She took the book they had given her and placed it on top of her smaller copy of Volume II. "I'll read them both as you suggest," she said, smiling.

They invited Eva to come again the following week, adding that attending gatherings helped a great deal with understanding certain aspects of the books, and getting to know people her age who were themselves friends of the Author was to her advantage. She agreed and promised to attend the following week.

On the way home, the children excitedly shared what they had done during their class, proudly showing Eva their paper crafts while sharing the theme of the day. Eva congratulated them for their paper puppets. The older lady in the van suggested Eva attend the Friday night gathering for young adults. Eva had never heard of such a thing. In her mind, the only thing young adults in Real Mountain wanted to do was go to the Zone or some other bar to get high or drunk or hook up with someone. At least that had been her reality for many years. She was more than curious to meet people her age who did not care for drunkenness or other things of that sort.

That same week, Eva tried to reconnect with Natasha. She spoke to her about the Author and the gatherings, but Natasha cut her short, saying she and George were not interested. They only wanted to focus on their studies to graduate with honours. She explained they would be moving to another city with better career opportunities for them upon graduation. They were one summer semester away from graduation, and they did not want any distractions, adding that the extra summer session was more demanding than any other.

As for the rest of her former friends, Eva did not make much effort to reconnect. She actually avoided them. They represented a life she no longer wanted, and having severed the ties a few years before, she was estranged from them. Eva was looking forward to meeting new friends her age at the Friday night gatherings.

The youth gatherings were similar to the Sunday morning gatherings, with music and a talk. However, the night's host was much younger and talked about issues that were relevant to young adults who were either still in university or new to the employment market. The host talked about how the Author's plan was for young adults to have integrity and display maturity even at a young age. The Author's love was palpable in the room and through the host's words. Eva felt fulfilled.

Weeks turned into months. Eva joined the music group as a backing vocalist. She faithfully attended Sunday mornings and Friday nights. The more she attended, the more she grew in her heart. The Author's words were making an impact on her life, to the point that Eva no longer felt lonely. The nasty voice that had nagged her for years was no longer speaking. The alarm bell she had heard in the past, that inner instinct that wanted to alert her when things were wrong or off, was also silenced. The transformation Eva exhibited was from the inside out. She was now hearing another type of voice, the inner voice that came from the Author's presence. She was slowly learning to listen to it and heed to His love.

Eva spent the summer enjoying her newly formed friendship with several girls and guys from the young adults' group. Nelly and Eva had become close friends. Nelly was different from Natasha, but her energy and enthusiasm were contagious. Nelly was to marry Dick, a guy from the gathering. They were deeply in love.

Eva spent much time with Nelly, who was a short, skinny blonde with blue eyes. She already had a toddler from a former relationship and was excited that Dick treated him as his own.

Eva was happy for Nelly and Dick, and almost envious of their union. She secretly asked the Author to bring into her life a man to love. For the first time, Eva wanted to love someone rather than feeling desperate to be loved by someone. She was so full of the Author's love that she felt like she was going to explode. She no longer felt a void, and the negative self-talk was gone.

At home, she sat down at her kitchen table and wrote a short list of non-negotiable attributes that her future mate needed to have. He had to be a friend of the Author. He couldn't drink alcohol, smoke, or take drugs. She included a few other items along that line but nothing more. Eva kept her list short to reflect only what mattered and trusted the Author to present her with the right man at the right time.

12

A TRUE FAIRY TALE

A s time passed, Eva felt more and more complete. The Author filled her heart with such
love that it was obvious for all to see. It trans-
ported her into a newness of life that she had
not known was possible. Her relationship with her parents
was improving rapidly. Eva alternated between attending her parents' gatherings in Myerbell and those in Real
Mountain. Peculiarly, every time she attended the Myerbell
gatherings, she looked around, hoping to see someone she
used to know from her school or a former neighbourhood,
and each time concluded with a bit of disappointment that
no one she used to know had met the Author.

One particular evening, Nelly told Eva that she wanted
to introduce her to Dick's best friend. Eva said she was not
interested, because the guy was not a friend of the Author.
Nelly insisted that it was as if he was, because he was such a
nice guy. But Eva stood firm in her convictions. Having had
her fair share of supposedly nice guys in her life, she was no
longer interested in another fiasco. She explained to Nelly
that her new life with the Author took priority over any other

relationships and that she did not want to pursue a relationship with a guy who did not understand that.

That fall, Eva spent all her weekends in Myerbell to be with her parents and attend the gatherings there. On an early November night, Nelly and Eva were chatting on the telephone. Nelly was excited to talk about her wedding colours, decorations, and floorplan. Her maid of honour would be her sister; Dick, being a single child, had asked his best friend to be his best man. Having become a friend of the Author himself over the past month, Nelly had noticed in him the positive transformation that a genuine surrender brings.

On the second weekend of November, Eva stayed in Real Mountain. After the gathering, she walked across the auditorium to the cute guy beside Nelly. It had to be Dick's closest friend. Only a few inches taller than Eva, Andrew had short dark hair, was muscular, with broad shoulders, and was handsome. Eva stretched out her hand to shake his.

"You must be Andrew. I'm Eva. Pleased to meet you."

He returned her smile "I'm pleased to meet you too."

Eva told the three of them that she had a previous engagement that afternoon, wished them a great day, and then left.

On her way out, she glanced at Andrew one more time. He was standing tall and strong beside Dick. Their eyes connected for a moment. Eva saw something in the way he looked at her. It was a look she had never seen in anyone else. The way he gazed at her was penetrating and genuine. There was a depth she could not shake as she left the building to meet Sean.

That afternoon, everything Sean said made no sense. By that time, they had been friends for a few years, and each conversation had always been positive and interesting.

However, that day was different. Everything seemed off. Sean would talk about things he liked and Eva realized they were things she did not care for at all. Eva suggested a viewpoint; Sean would oppose it. It was as if they were suddenly in different camps debating their opinions like two opposing political parties at a legislative assembly.

When Eva got home that evening, it was clear to her that Sean was not someone she wanted to marry. She called Nelly. The two girls were giggly and excited like two toddlers on Christmas Eve. Eva was interested in getting to know Andrew better and hoped he felt the same way, even though their first encounter had been less than brief, to say the least. It was agreed that, on Wednesday, Eva would have dinner with Nelly, Dick, and Andrew at Dick's place.

That Wednesday after work, Eva took a city transit bus and exited at the bus stop nearest Dick's apartment. Noticing Andrew on the other side of the street, she crossed at the green light. As she walked toward Andrew, a sweet, still voice whispered in her heart. *Eva, meet your husband.* That inner voice, which played the role of an alarm bell that she had tried to shut up for so long, was now free to speak when necessary. And right now it was singing a joyful, heavenly song.

Andrew presented her with a rose as she took his arm. He had been mandated by Nelly to pick her up at the bus stop to bring her to Dick's apartment, which was located in an amalgam of new building complexes that all looked identical to each other. As they walked toward the apartment building, Andrew and Eva engaged in a conversation as if they had known each other for ten years. It was surreal. The peace that flowed between them was refreshing. Eva had never experienced it with anyone.

Dinner was fun. They enjoyed a good meal, and Nelly's three-year-old son was the centre of attention. His naiveté was sweet and warmed the heart. Eva took the dishes from the dining room table to the kitchen sink and helped Andrew clean up. On the refrigerator, a magnet held a telephone bill with the name "Andrew Kasteyou."

Hmm . . . Eva Kasteyou. I like the sound of that!

Eva and Andrew spent the following evening with Dick, Nelly, and her son. On Friday night, Dick and Andrew were scheduled to play hockey. Dick, Nelly, and her son headed to the arena together, while Andrew and Eva stayed behind at Dick's apartment to talk further before leaving. They never made it to the game. That night, Andrew told Eva how much in awe he was that the Author had enabled them to meet. He added that Eva was nothing like the girls he had dated in the past.

Eva was equally stunned by Andrew's positive qualities. She had never dreamed that a man like him might exist. They talked about the importance of the Author in their life and how attending the gatherings had transformed them. They shared their dreams and aspirations for the future and were thrilled to find out how similar they were. They also shared their first kiss. Eva was floating on Cloud Nine.

They spent the entire weekend together. However, each night Eva went home, because they both agreed they would keep themselves for marriage.

That Sunday night was a special gathering where people shared what the Author had done in their life. Having had that experience several months earlier, Eva was now part of the audience of about 100. They all wanted to hear the new friends of the Author tell their story about how the Author had impacted their life. Now it was Andrew's turn.

The host asked what the Author had done in his life, and Andrew shared how the Author had led him to his future wife. Everyone cheered and clapped with joy and approval. Eva was thrilled. Although she knew in her heart from the moment she crossed the street that Andrew would be her husband, it warmed her heart that a man would publicly declare her to be the woman of his dreams. And she was touched that everyone expressed their approval. Her new spiritual family was testifying openly that Eva and Andrew were meant for each other.

Eva's experience in her current relationship was different from every other relationship she'd had. Every cell of her being acknowledged that Andrew was the man of her dreams, the man with whom she would spend the rest of her life. Even though she had met him only the week before, he was her Prince Charming, her knight in shining armour, her valiant musketeer. The Author made their union possible. Without the Author, they would have never met. Eva was so grateful.

A few weeks later, Eva and Andrew drove to Myerbell to meet her parents, who warmly welcomed Andrew into the family. For the first time, Eva's father liked her boyfriend. In the past, Eva had brought several boyfriends to her parents and to family celebrations. Either her father tolerated her beaus or disliked them altogether. But with Andrew, it was love at first sight. After they left, Eva's parents agreed that they had just met their future son-in-law, as the Author testified in their heart.

On December 23, during a gathering, Andrew went up to the stage and, in front of everyone, asked Eva to marry him. She agreed with much joy but no surprise. They had talked about it at great length and knew it was what they both wanted.

Two days later, Eva presented Andrew as her fiancé to the entire family for the first time. Uncles, aunts, and cousins greeted him politely, with no particular excess of joy.

Her godfather took Eva's parents aside and said what everyone was thinking. "You're not going to let her marry this guy, are you? She doesn't even know him. She changes boyfriends like she changes shirts! That's not going to last. She should live with him for a while first to see if this is serious. What is she thinking?"

With the Author's peace, Eva's parents lovingly responded that Eva was now of age to make this kind of decision on her own and encouraged her godfather to get to know Andrew better before making assumptions. They added that, statistically speaking, there was no better chances of success in marriage for couples who lived together first.

Eva's parents knew her godfather was not a friend of the Author; therefore, he would not understand their internal witness. Joining the rest of the family, the trio did not engage any further in discussion.

By the end of January, all the planning for the March 30, wedding was complete. No longer having preparations to keep them busy, Andrew and Eva started to struggle with their mutual promise to wait for marriage before becoming intimate. Their kissing was passionate, and saying goodbye in the car took longer and longer each day. Eva kept accountable to her mother and Nelly. At some point, Andrew and Eva agreed they could not even kiss anymore if they wanted to keep their promise to each other. Eva's mother laughingly recommended Eva take cold showers. Nelly suggested staying in groups or in public places as much as possible to avoid temptation.

For Andrew and Eva, this was a matter of honouring their word. If they could not honour their word before marriage, how could they trust their word would be kept after? They understood that their decision was countercultural, and those who didn't understand the principles taught in the Author's book would laugh in derision. They didn't mind what everyone else said or thought. Only what the Author thought mattered. They knew they were honouring Him first, which had a ripple effect of honouring each other.

In mid-February, they found an apartment they both liked. The owner was a friend of Andrew's, and he agreed to rent beginning the first of April, though they could start moving their things in a week before. Having given notice to each their landlords, they started to pack their things. That last week was filled with anticipation. They gave a fresh coat of paint to all the rooms of the two-bedroom basement apartment and started to organize their things.

On March 29, everything was moved in and ready. That night, they each slept at their parents' houses. After what felt like the longest four and a half months of their existence, Andrew and Eva were finally getting married.

The next morning, Eva awoke with a sense of peace that transcended her personality. Usually bubbly and easily excitable, she lay on the couch calmly. Eating breakfast with her parents was different now that Eva was an adult and the three of them shared the same inner experience. The Author had saved their lives, and the book answered all their questions. The unrest that Eva had felt throughout her teenage years had vanished. She no longer lingered in self-hatred. She could now interact with her parents in a responsible and mature way. Breakfast was Eva's favourite: buckwheat pancakes with maple syrup.

Then there were the hair and nail appointments. Having eaten lunch on the sly, it was time to put on her beautiful white wedding gown. It fit Eva perfectly. It was made of white silk and had a long train at the back. Her veil surrounded her head and neck all the way to the middle of her back and chest. It was attached to a tiara. She put on her Cinderella-like white silk shoes. The length of her white gloves provided coverage up to her upper arms, only a few inches away from the short sleeves of her dress. The pearl earrings she and her mother had purchased provided the final touch.

The limousine waited at the door. The long drive to Real Mountain Gathering Hall enabled tears of joy and chatters of excitement. Everyone was dressed warmly, as the early spring could only provide a meagre twelve degrees Celsius. A few clouds were dancing in the blue sky. It was a beautiful day.

Fashionably late, Eva entered the building. The decorations were simple yet beautiful. Uncles, aunts, and cousins from both sides were waiting for the grand overture of the event.

Eva's family had warmed up to Andrew. In the months preceding, he had proven to be a trustworthy, mature, and likeable individual. His calm, level-headed nature was reassuring. Eva being the first of the grandchildren to get married, everyone in the family was there.

Eva and Andrew had eyes only for each other. While the man performing the marriage was talking to them about the importance of this commitment and how it had been ordained by the Author, they were googly eyed and whispering in each other's ears how much they loved each other and how beautiful the other was, so much so that the man, realizing they were not listening to him, turned to the crowd and candidly declared, "There's popcorn at the back," causing everyone to burst into laughter.

After publicly declaring their love and commitment to each other, and the famous "you may kiss the bride" was said, Eva and Andrew French-kissed passionately. Everyone clapped and cheered. Eva and Andrew kept kissing, and the family continued to clap and cheer, to the point of being uncomfortable. Everyone started to laugh in discomfort while the two lovebirds, oblivious to their surroundings, persisted in kissing. Even though everyone thought it, no one dared to say, "Get a room!" That day, all agreed this had been the most unusual wedding they ever attended.

After the traditional human tunnel was formed by the members of both families, from the auditorium to the outside door, everyone joining hands in the air for the bride and groom to walk under. At its end, Eva and Andrew entered the limousine. The last of the pictures for that part of the day were taken, and then off they went, leading the procession to the second part of the evening, the party.

The banquet hall was nicely decorated, and a bottle of wine, provided by Andrew's parents, adorned each table. The presence of the red liquid resulted from a conversation between Andrew and his father. While planning their wedding, Andrew informed his father there would not be any alcohol at the banquet. His father opposed the idea, suggesting a cash bar, where those wishing to drink could pay for their own. Andrew conceded, but made it clear that he did not want to spend any money on alcohol, particularly now that he had decided to no longer indulge in the habit. His father insisted that a wedding was not a wedding without wine on the table to complement the meal. Puzzled by his son's new convictions on the matter, he offered to pay for the bottles, adding that it would be his wedding gift. Andrew conceded gracefully, not wanting to displease his father, who already had mixed feeling about his son attending gatherings.

Eva's parents sat next to her at the table of honour while Andrew's parents sat next to him.

During the main course, Eva's parents stood up and addressed the newlyweds. "Now observe carefully how things are properly done," her father said. To Eva's surprise and amazement, he passionately kissed his wife while everyone whistled and clapped cheerfully. Eva was blown away by the transformation the Author had performed on her father. She barely recognized him. She could see how much he had been freed from so many fears, particularly fears of demonstrating affection.

The traditional glass clinking for the newlyweds to kiss took place, and family members sang love songs to get more kisses from them. The atmosphere was joyful, as if the Author had created a protective bubble over everyone in the hall to preserve everyone's memories of the hurts, grudges, and bitterness of the past. There was a freedom in the air that could not be explained but was experienced in a palpable way.

After the wedding cake was cut and everyone had indulged in the homemade dessert, it was time for the bride and groom to open the floor with the first dance. A song about a love that is endless was played, and the new couple floated in each other's arms. Both sets of parents joined in, and then other family members filled the dance floor. Eva also enjoyed a dance with her father. As they danced, he told her how proud he was of her. It warmed her heart, because she knew he was sincere and speaking from the heart.

Andrew and Eva left in the limousine shortly after to head toward the most prestigious hotel in Real Mountain. Spending the honeymoon night in one of their wedding suites was romantic.

In the wee hours of the morning, they headed to the airport for a one-week honeymoon in Jamaica. Running away from the cold temperatures at the end of winter was a delight and finally being alone day and night with her Prince Charming was soothing for Eva. They had accomplished what practically no one did. They kept a promise the rest of the world mocked or even loathed. They waited until marriage to be intimate, and it proved to be rewarding.

For eternity, Eva would be able to look in the eyes of her beloved and see a man who respected her until marriage. For eternity, Eva would be able to stand next to a man who kept his promises. For eternity, Eva could boast that her husband was a man of integrity and honour. Their intimacy was based on mutual respect, commitment, and faithfulness, and the Author was there to help them keep it that way. The Author was leading them, guiding them, and filling them. Andrew loved the Author more than he loved Eva, and Eva loved the Author more than she loved Andrew. Each desired to please Him, love Him, and aspire to get closer to Him with every breath. Automatically, it made them love each other more and grow closer to each other. Their identity was with the Author, not with each other. Because of this, the demand for the other to fill the gap or inner void was a non-issue. It was the Author's job. When strife, misunderstanding, or arguments hit their relationship, they both went to the Author for help. Each time the Author faithfully counselled them on the right path. The more they obeyed Him by following in His footsteps, the more their life blossomed and was freed. The chains of slavery from addictions, low self-esteem, worry, anxiety, and people-pleasing were taken off one by one.

And they lived happily ever after.

 Printed in Canada